PANOPTICON

For the intense yearning which each of them has towards the other, does not appear to be the desire of lover's intercourse, but of something else which the soul of either evidently desires and cannot tell, and of which she has only a dark and doubtful presentiment.

PLATO: *The Symposium*

UNA CREMA PARA EL ACNE UNA LOCION UN ASTRINGENTE DE PAPEL PERFILADOR DE OJOS LAPIZ DE OJOS TOALLITAS DE MAQUILLAJE LACA ESMALTE DE UNAS POLVOS COLORANTE TINTE ACEITE LACA TIJERAS DE UNAS MANOPLA DE FELPA JABON ESPONJA PINZAS PAPEL HIGIENCO

puede darme ...

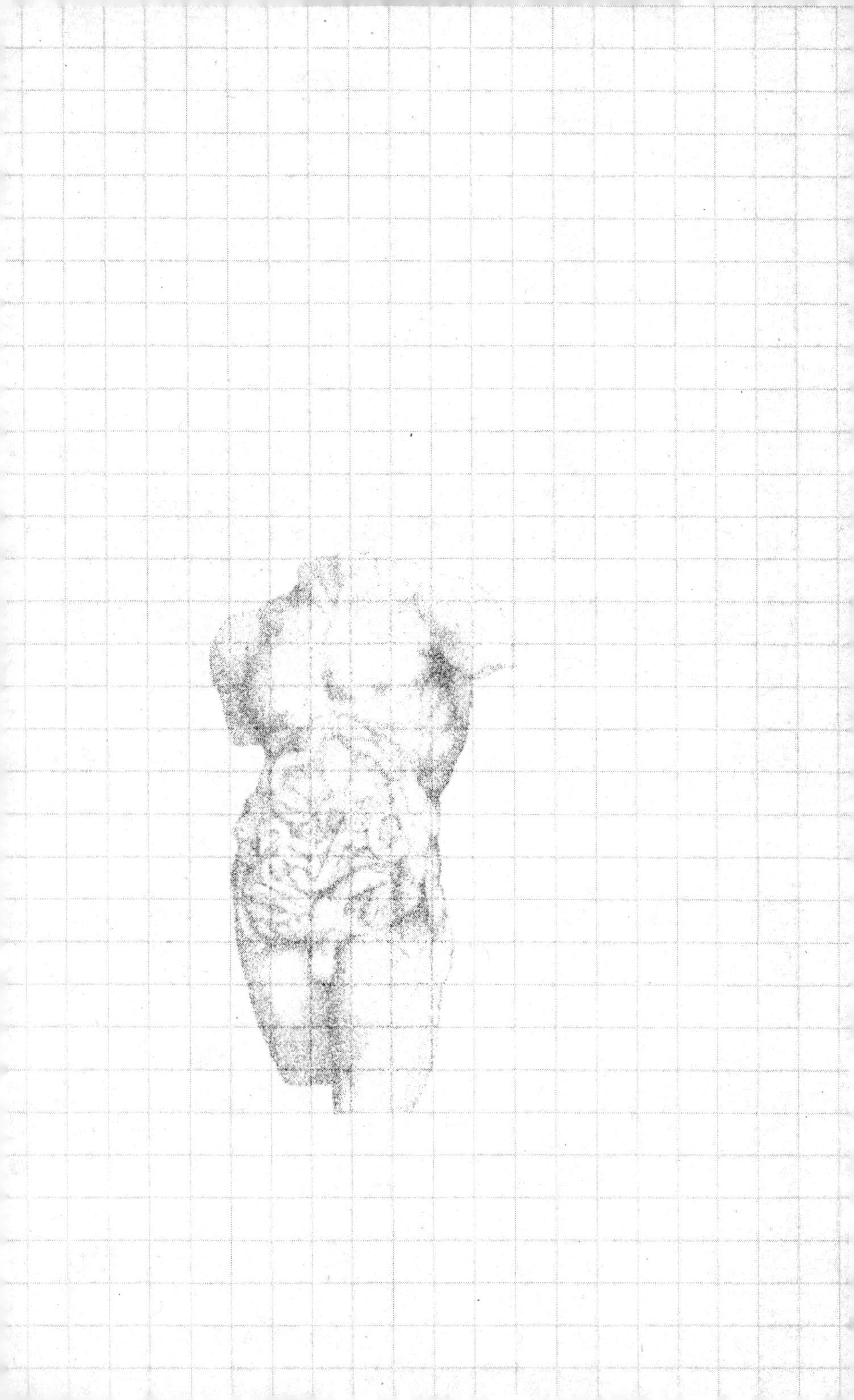

A WOMAN EMERGES FROM HER BATH TOWELS HERSELF DRY AND COMMENCES DRESSING. IN THE TIME TAKEN FOR THE PHOTOGRAPHER TO MOVE FROM THE ROSE-WOOD ESCRITOIRE TO THE BATHROOM DOOR THE WOMAN REACHES FOR A SILVER OBJECT (A BRACELET POSSIBLY OR A RING) AND PLACES THIS ON HER BODY. SHE HAS ASSUMED THE PERSONA OF AN AGING MOVIE STAR IN A FILM CALLED "THE MARK." SHE REACHES OVER FOR A NOVEL SHELVED BY THE EDGE OF THE BATH. IN THE PHOTOGRAPH THE PHOTOGRAPHER TAKES THE TITLE OF THIS BOOK IS CLEARLY VISIBLE: "THE MIND OF PAULINE BRAIN." AS SHE READS SHE IS REMEMBERING A RECENT TRANSPOSITION OF THE BOOK INTO A FILM SCRIPT. (THE FILM IS TO BE SHOT NEXT MONTH ON LO-CATION IN SPAIN WITH A MODEST BUDGET.) SHE REMEM-BERS TOO THAT THROUGH ALL OF THIS THERE IS THE DISTINCT SOUND OF SOMEONE TYPING.

DEPARTMENT OF REISSUE NO. 7

PANOPTICON

STEVE McCAFFERY

BOOKTHUG | TORONTO, 2011

FIRST BOOKTHUG EDITION

The production of this book was made possible through the generous assistance of the Canada Council for the Arts and the Ontario Arts Council.

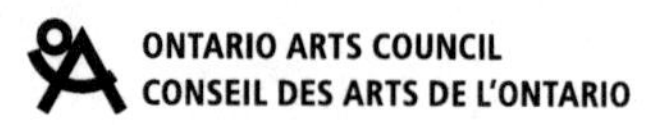

Printed in Canada.

Library and Archives Canada Cataloguing in Publication

McCaffery, Steve
Panopticon / Steve McCaffery.

(Department of reissue ; no. 7)
Originally publ.: Toronto : blewointmentpress, 1984.
ISBN 978-1-897388-91-4

I. Title. II. Series: Department of reissue ; no. 7

PS8575.C33P25 2011 C813'.54 C2011-904772-1

for Karen ... still ... and more so

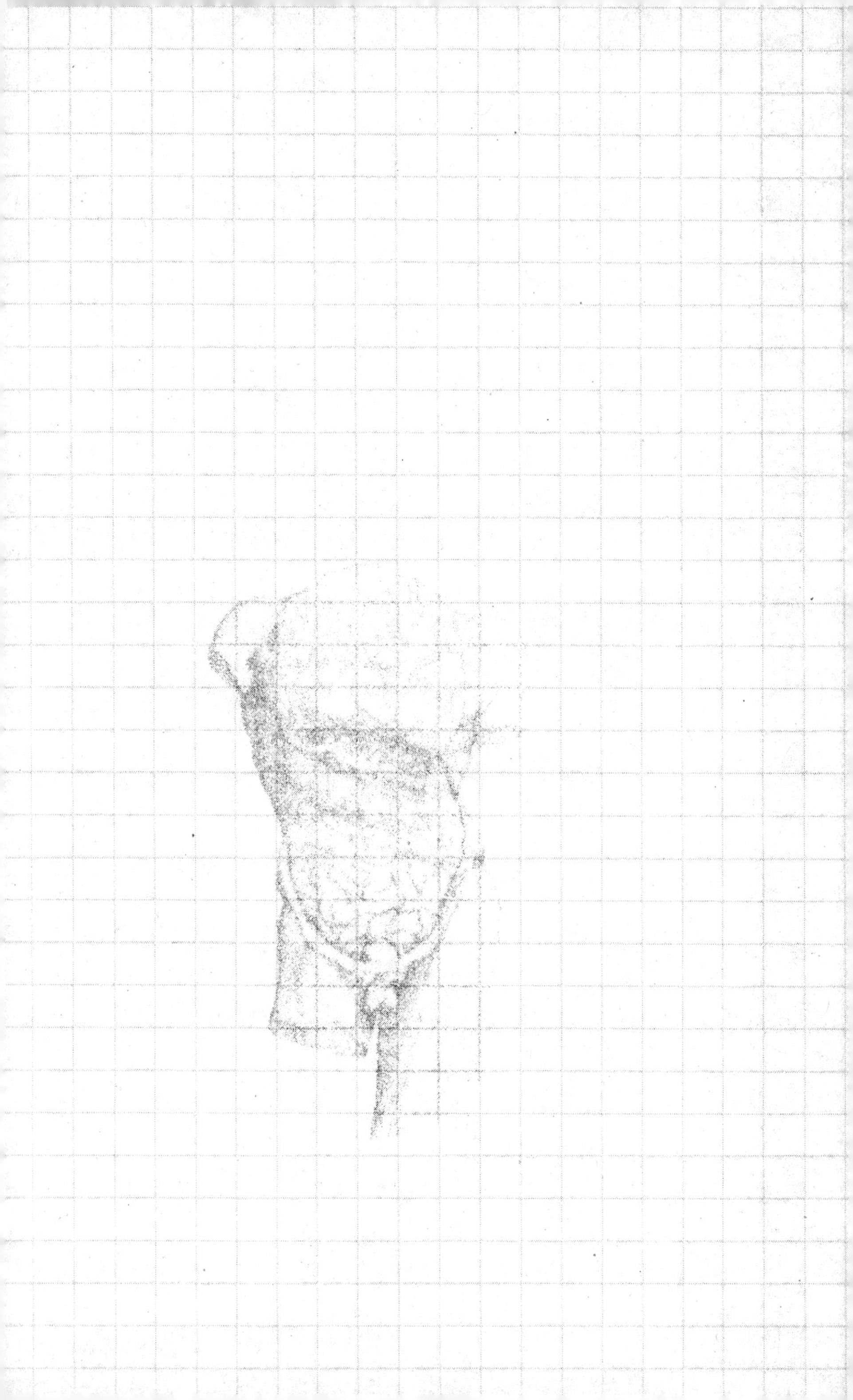

eras amet qui nunquam amavit quique amavit cras amet

Pervigilium Veneris

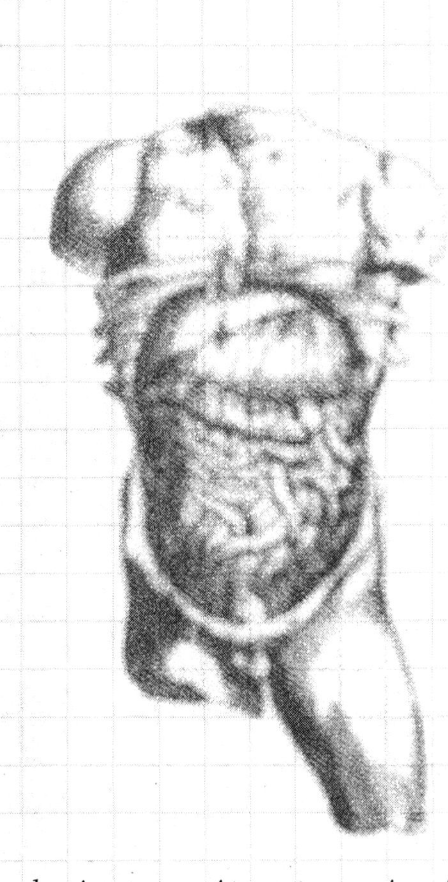

homines qouque si taceant, vocem invenient libri

Inscr. Guilferbylanae Bibliothecae

PLATES 21–39

The focus moves to a woman writing. She is middle aged. Her pen plastic. The focus moves to a woman reading. She is middle aged. Her hair wet. Across her left shoulder is a towel. In front of her is a list. Reading another page in silence. From the radio comes fragments of human conversation. The reception is weak and the conversation frequently fades. There is a pause in the reading. Some words get lost. There is something spoken about night, about intellectual luminosity and wounds "and in the night despite our lamps and listenings despite the intellectual attempts at brilliance the dark space comes on us unpronounceable, unidentifiable in words that cut and mix into a permanent wound the hot scars of a chlorotic moon viewed by the two of us together as we sit here on the frontiers of a mind assassinating habits." The focus moves to a section of the page. No clear words are discernible. The rapid movement of the head over the page causes a sequence of words to form as missive loops and spools, a curious analogy to wired circuits or pubic hairs. At some point between the image of the chlorotic moon and the phrase "missive loops and spools" the woman's voice may become audible through any one of three available citations:

1. “There is a pornography that splits its words into the plazas of your mediocre recyclings, re-births, retirements from the habitudes of men or small girls in frocks displaced familial friggings tied by the severer loops of an inner guilt to
—Shush, this is only your father’s tongue and this will be our secret.”

2. “They are all impossible despairs, designs perpetuated by that exclusivity of mirror spaced to dissipate horizons.”

3. “We call the body sex for lack of a dirtier word. But cocks on large dogs attain the greatest freedom. When a man drinks alone then nothing will happen. If children appear you abolish them quick. It is from my body that I write these words to formulate the image of an anus, that terrible dog’s eye becoming a mouth to formulate its dogma. It is from my body that I wish to speak so that the words won’t disgust. For example, instinct is an axiom for general exemption from the risible rules of nuance. For example, revolution is an architecture where the pale drunks puke in sight of us. There is nothing but pleasure, interrelationship and problems.”

But two citations are disallowed:

1. “Every horizon we ever visited had its own gas station and none of them was ever closed. You see, this is still a pose behind words, but also a position within them. And to fix the eye in its own definition we must remember sight is

that which we cannot speak."

2. "A woman emerges from her bath towels herself dry and begins dressing. In the space of the next few minutes she reaches for a silver object a bracelet or perhaps a ring and places it on her body. She has assumed the persona of a movie star as she reaches over for a novel shelved at the foot of her bed. Its title is "The Mark." As she reads she remembers the film described in another book called "The Mind of Pauline Brain." It starts with the image of a woman reading. She is middle aged. Her hair wet. In front of her is a list. A man (the killer in the story) emerges from a room and reaches for a knife (a book in the original draft). There is a sound through all of this of someone typing. The focus moves to the source of that sound. It is the woman who previously had written the list the woman now has in front of her. She is middle aged. Across her left shoulder is a towel. In the space of the next few minutes she reaches for a silver object and places it around her neck. There are marks to suggest an earlier struggle. The man (the killer in the film within the story) stops, adjusts his spectacles and reads a small note that has caught his eye. In the carriage of the typewriter is the woman's own scenario. Another shorter note contains two solitary words written in Spanish: incommunicable parole."

Part III

THE MIND OF PAULINE BRAIN

Eradicate the name, the character, the entire action and substitute the structural zones of clinical and critical discourse and she'll still be there. Though displaced she was not annihilated. She became fixed, as remote control, in the systemes of the anti-model. And that room became her own gynocracy. She is the space of her own absence and she will always be there as the proper name never spoken.

Repetition of the paragraph commencing "I concluded with ..."
I CONCLUDED WITH A FURTHER DISPLACEMENT INTO ENIGMA. THROUGH THE HISTORICAL FIELD OF INTERROGATION I PASSED INTO THE PROBLEMATIC ARENA OF AN ANSWER FROM THE OUTSIDE. I WAS NOT EXACTLY THE OTHER, MORE THE PATHETIC SUM OF ERRORS OF A NAME. SO I SHIFT AS YOU SHIFT ME BUT THE DRIFT'S THE SAME. I AM ALWAYS ELSEWHERE FORMED INVIOLABLE IN WHATEVER FORM IS REIFIED. BEYOND CONTAMINATION.

In the sum of her emergences from all her baths and towellings, in that general pestilence called meaning, in the words she is, she stays the writing writing this, transcendent, immobile, a sovereign presence in a lack of being, repeating a phrase concluding with "the general trajectory of a circle."

WE LEARN THAT THE FACT OF ABSENCE IS OVERWHELMING THAT THE EVOLUTION TOWARDS MADNESS LEADS INTO A SUDDEN MUTATION TO THE WHOLE THE STATIC AND THE COHERENT. FOR IT IS WRITTEN THAT IT SAYS WHEN HE IS IN HER SHE IS SOMEWHERE ELSE. EXISTENCE. HENCE THE UNITY WE FIND POSTERIOR TO THE DISSOCIATION. LIFE SEX DEATH YIELD WORDS THAT EXTEND BEYOND THEMSELVES AND BEYOND THE PROBLEMATIC COLLISEUMS OF ONE MIND'S OWN MIRRORS. CALL IT PSEUDOPSYCHOARCHAEOLOGY YET WE STILL HAVEN'T DISSOCIATED THE TEXT FROM ALL ORDERS OF MORALS. THE DEAD HAVE FUCKED THE LIVING IN A BODY RENDERED THEATRE, YET THE FRAGMENTATION OF THAT FLESH HAS SETTLED IN THE PROLEGOMENON OF THE MARK. THERE IS NO FILM BY THAT NAME. NO BOOK. ONLY A THEFT OF YOURSELF FROM YOURSELF ALONG THE GENERAL TRAJECTORY OF A CIRCLE.

Repetition of the paragraph: "The sterility of having nothing to say. And then a smile. I must first hear myself laugh. I must hear myself in that gesture which, beyond my own name, marks me for repetition. Recognition in the act i become when whoever hears me sees me arrive. In a fugitive tense. The very nomad."

THE STERILITY OF HAVING NOTHING TO SAY. AND THEN A SMILE. I MUST FIRST HEAR MYSELF LAUGH. I MUST HEAR MYSELF IN THAT GESTURE WHICH, BEYOND MY

OWN NAME, MARKS ME FOR REPETITION. RECOGNITION IN THE ACT I BECOME WHEN WHOEVER HEARS ME SEES ME ARRIVE. IN A FUGITIVE TENSE. THE VERY NOMAD.

From this point on in the pronoun there can be no return and equally no departure. As the categories break her up you step aside into the moment you decide to write on out of the nightmare that attends you. Nothing is left you. Not even fear. What you desire stays away from you. Unresponsive. Not even haunting. A WOMAN EMERGES FROM HER BATH ETC. AND STEPS INTO A MARK THAT'S BIGGER THAN ALL HER MEANINGS. Something like that. Something about a single sentence bringing about a cause in which a body dries itself. A little like life. "And the dark night around the doorbell spans this truth until the light explodes expanding both minds to that devotion which expunges all criteria."

The light which addresses me is not the same light which attracts the coloured smock I'm wearing. Nor the light cast on the old hat you wore previous to the mixing of those starts:

I have just returned from a visit to a movie ...
A woman emerges from her bath towels herself dry and begins dressing ...

In a broader sense it is the light cast on all objective identities "as when the woman still sits reading a woman middle aged who holds a pen and reaches for a book shelved by the escritoire." All these are the places of stammering discovered to be endless or the cogitations in a dream about not journeying. Obedient, she runs the risk that pure grammar has become a certainty posed as a question.

The roundness of your face is the example. Some remain as they are notched by not thinking how the marks erase as they are made the marks that run across or run between as it is sometimes said the letters are. Written by the photographs developed in haste.

With theory standing for the teeth the eyes aren't geometry anymore. Blind surfaces are lines, rigid lines get bent, lines (ideas) curve their morphologies (the curves your mother insisted would repair themselves in time) the factual shapes of the forms stood for by the hand.

Correction: Who can count the gradations of sensible intuition or the accidental vague amorphous rumblings of a narwhal through vaginal waters thoughts in that neighbourhood urethra sphincter stirrings stirred alone and scattered in remorse.

We accuse of practical control and this lapse in the rigor of the corporeal (the simple statement that her wounds have healed) we commit to a scenario.

Again and again. And so on. And so forth. And back again. And once more. And one more time. Again and again and through and through. Over and over again and again. Moments anticipatory. Then cancelled. And then again. And again and again. And over and over. Anticipatory of. And then the passages the limits. And then beyond them. Then erased. And again and again. Repetition of. A thousand times. Then more or less. Or a little more. Then more. And smaller then smaller and on and on. And then again and again and still yet again. And further. And moreover. And even so the sun the region the unity the declension the former the forgetting the penultimate. To be remembered and recalled. And yet again not again. And on and on until the abstract the madness the moment of both. And nothing. And so on and so on. And even more. And yet again. And still further. And further to that. And that. And more than that. And even more and nonetheless the self the blindness the self in the blindness the touch the repeating the sameness where you bring yourself to display yourself and stand and stand there and stand again and stay in that spot and remain there and over there and here and more so there and still there and so and so on and so on and on and on and onward and more and more beyond more and more beyond itself and beyond that to there and beyond there to here and beyond here to the phrase "it's difficult to admit that it's broken apart, finished, over, ended before we really ever gave it a chance" and following the phrase "and yes, i know that in a way it's tragic yet in a way it's a blessing" and on and not on and then beyond there to here and beyond here to the phrase "yes, it seems so very strange" and on and not on until another phrase and another and still another until the phrase "it's something like all that's relative to what you know" and on and on and later and later still and still another and another until the phrase "i wish you wouldn't" and later and later on and over there to the phrase "it really doesn't concern you" and after a while a space and yet again and no less than this and then that phrase the missing phrase the phrase to end it the phrase to shift from place to over there to somewhere else to other than here the phrase which ends with "yes, i know, the logic reawakens" and then sleep and then asleep again and again and in others in your arms up to the phrase "please hold me" and other than you and him and her and other than inside him and all of them and then the loss and then the forgetting more and then and moreover and over again forgetting more and then and moreover and over again and even less than this and less again and again and on and on through to the focus the vitality the moment lost the loss caught in the phrase "yes i know as well" then the transit in distinct suspension nothing heard nothing said nothing mentioned nothing beyond it fixed then held then holding on to held against and on and on and longer and no longer till impossible till inappropriate and banal then jejeune and then renegade and then abortive or subjective the sediments the casings of the germs of the names out of mind out of frame with no attitude no plenitude no presence some jam a few eggs a little bread and more jam some presence he is speaking some tea he is speaking then the words then the phrase then goodbye i have to go i have to return i am here on a visit nothing more nothing less nothing else a little food a little more tea a little thanks a little cheese no cheese no phrase no repetition only you only us only them in a fact in a phrase in a new sense a being and so on a lasting and so on to where it stops eventually to where it removes to where it alters and where it goes and why the symptoms and this and that and only now and never here and never there and again and once more the totality the isolation the total lack the presence the being the phrase the soliloquy. And this. And still this. And still this. A single eye. And still more. A pupil. And more. The eye. The tooth. And more. And then and only then. And the hand. And the other hand and yet again. And then a single eye. And another. Then a rest and a pause and then on. Then a gland. And more. Then a glove. And more. And then a phrase "how human being is a system." Never truth. Supposing that. Never real. Supposing that. Never ultimate. Supposing that. Then again. Supposing that. But then again. Then a why. Then a meanwhile. Then a during. Supposing that. Then a there. Supposing that. And as well. Supposing that. Then as well. Supposing that. Then again and then against and why and where they go and why truth and why woman. Supposing that. And never she never he never them never names. Supposing that. Never themes. And then again. Never corpus never pretext never tossed never spurred never difference. Supposing that. Then as well. Supposing style. The style alone. That style alone. That system style alone and by itself. Supposing that. In isolate. That style alone. And then again. The woman style. And then again. The truth style. Supposing that. Suppose that style and then again. And through the man.

How the woman when the man because the woman in spite the man. In his sex. Supposing that. Never he. In her sex. Never that. Never he never him never in never with never beside never instead of. Then as well. And again. Never us. And again. Supposing woman. And the style. And the surface. Man. And the reading. Woman. And the action. Man. And then the questions. The transgression. Woman. Supposing asterisks. To mark her. To style her. So that a question leaps from where she smiles. Supposing. From where he sits. Supposing. From where she reads. Supposing style. The smile. The fruit. The challenge. The intimacy. Supposing that. Outside the smile. Imagine that. Outside the room. A single tooth. Imagine that. Only a surface. Imagine. Only a laughter. Imagine. Repetition of the phrase "shush it's only the children walking by." Supposing that. Supposing a pause. Repetition of the phrase "nothing new will occur." A moment. Doing. Another moment. Proving. Another moment. Reaching. Another moment. Attaining. Another moment. Grasping. Another moment. Stabbing. Another moment. Talking. Another moment. Sucking. Another moment. Spitting. Another moment. Removing. Another moment. Repetition of the phrase "nothing new under the sun." And then again. And again. And further on. And more. And further more. And still more. Convinced. Perhaps. Certain. Perhaps. Then a detour. Supposing that. Then a road renamed. Supposing that. Then a definition. Redefined filled with water. Then the history of drowning boys in the culminating phrase "I'm sorry love, nihilism doesn't allow you further cigarettes." Supposing that. And further times. And further spaces. And further jaundice. Imagine that. Then gender. Then voice. Then figuration. And then admission. Supposing that. Then a woman. And going round. And then a man. And then women. And then three men.

As they are. And going round. And coming back. Towards three men. Towards feelings. Towards style. Perhaps error. And sure. And forgetting. And forgiving. Supposing that. Then allowing a question. Then along. Then back. Towards a question. Circling around the question. Tentative steps around the question. And then again. Disproval admission argument abuse until abatement. Tenebrosities. Artifacts. Totems. Legendary deeds. Needing children. Needing sex. In what is called love. Imagine that. In what is called property. Who knows. Surrender. Who knows. A scheme. A martyrdom. A defect a passion a rubric a skill from the head that speaks of rights. Imagine that. Of human warmth. Of dispositions pathos renunciations abyss and mercy. Imagine that. From the heat. An attack. Supposing that. Until the time. And then. Until the space. And then again. The mood. And then again. The rhythm turned returned tuned in unconditional. The eyes. And then again. The stimmung. Manifest. Dyadic. Out of love. Imagine that. Into love between moments. Between starts. Between phrases. Repetition of "i love you." Repetition of "i can't go on." And then the turbulence. And then the cold. A glass a warming phrase. Repetition of "i really love you." And then the horror of a vacuum never ending never there never fixed. Supposing that. Suppose that concept. That possession that ideal such good. Authentic. Time. Authentic. Movement. Genuine peace. The love. The child. False. Supposing that. Imagine children. And of home. And of what is proper what is presence what is gift. Of a sort. Imagine. Of a sort not specified. But something vague. Just suppose. Something vague. That orifice. Imagine. Just suppose. The shout. The scream. Then movement. Authentic. Just suppose. The paradox. The proof that proves itself to be. The gift. Or lack of. The sperm. Or lack of. The peace. Or lack of. The eye. Or lack of. The gift the charity lack of need lack of time. Lots of time. Inasmuch. Lots of time. Just suppose. In as much. Just imagine. And so on. And so forth. And on and again and so again accorded out of reach. Just imagine. Out of incidence. In as much as. Out of need. Just suppose. And so on. And the meaning. And the question. And the space. Just imagine. And the hesitation. Then movement. Or lack. Then orifice. Or lack. And so on. And so forth. A single eye. A fixed ambition. Repetition of the phrase "i really didn't want it to end like this." In as much as. Then itself. Then some other. Repetition of the phrase "yes, i know, i feel the same i feel i'd like to give it another try." Just imagine. Out of need. In as much as. The single eye. Repetition of the phrase "a voluntary victim." And so on. Repetition of the phrase "i forgot my purse." Repetition of the phrase "it's useless." Repetition of the phrase "yes it was a useless thing to do." And the light and the certitude and the letter from the friend. Just imagine. And your mother. Just imagine. And your mother's friend. And so on. And the letter. And so on. Repetition of the phrase "he died three years ago." Just imagine. A woman. Just imagine. Repetition of the phrase "the movie is all about death in a certain way about life too." And the aphorism. And the starts at being friends. And what she brought. And what she erected. Repetition of the phrase "fecal matter." Repetition of the phrase "your mother's wish." And so on. And again. And again. In the phrase. Repeated endlessly. Just imagine. In the phrase. In as much as. In the phrase. Repeated endlessly. Just imagine. Without ceasing. Just imagine. And so on. Time and again. And so on. Time in and time out. And so on. And on and on. Time after time. The phrase repeated. And again. The phrase repeated beginning "iterations of fecal memories." Just imagine. That had no place. Imagine. Had no time. Had no register. No effect. Time and again. No means to gather. Time and again. No fact behind it. Endlessly. No frame. Utterly. Just imagine. Utterly. Repetition of the phrase “the voluntary doings of a victim.” Time and again. Day after day. The phrase repeated. Minute by minute. Night after night. Time in and time out. The light from the hill. Just imagine. That church in the movie. Brick by brick. That had no place. No sentence. The phrase repeated. Day after day. Imagine that. Endlessly. Hour by hour. Endlessly. That had no fact behind it. The phrase repeated. Just imagine. On and on. Second by second. Just imagine. The description. Inasmuch as. The victim. In as much as. Description. In as much as. The victim. And the phrase “the way she gave confession.” And the phrase “yes, i guess we have to admit.” And on and

on and on and on and on and on and on and on and on and on
and on and on and on and on and on and on and on and on and
on and on and on and on and on and on and on and on and on
and on and on and on and on and on and on and on and on and
on and on and on and on and on and on and on and on and on
and on and on and on and on and on and on and on and on and
on and on and on and on and on and on and on and on and on
and on and on and on and on and on and on and on and no and
on and on and on and on and on and on and on and on and on
and on and on and on and on and on and on and on and on and
on and on and on and on and on and on and on and on and on
and on and on and on and on and on and on and on and on and
on and on and on and on and on and on and on and on and on
and on and on and on and on and on and on and on and on and
on and on and on and on and on and on and on and on and on
and on and on and on and on and on and on and on and on and
on and on and on and on and on and on and on and on and on
and on and on and on and on and on and on and on and on and
on and on and on and on and on and on and on and on and on
and on and on and on and on and on and on and on and on and
on and on and on and on and on and on and on and on and on
and on and on and on and on and on and on and no and on and
on and on and on and on and on and on and on and on and on
and on and on and on and on and on and on and on and on and
on and on and on and on and on and on and on and on and on
and on and on and on and on and on and on and on and on and
on and on and on and on and on and on and on and on and on

PLATES 43–82

Description of a man (the hero, the killer or the killer's lawyer) replacing a book upon a shelf. Room is probably a study of some kind, several piles of paper, unsorted index cards, a cold, half-drunk cup of tea. Yellow fragments of typewriter correcting tape. A pencil with a broken tip. The man is not alone. Distant sound of typing fusing with sound of running bath water. A woman's voice from a familiar stanza. Man sits down at a chair and sorts through papers spread out before him. Movie ends. Title: *The Mark.* They leave the cinema and walk east a few blocks towards the phrase "a parked car." As they reach it he notices a small pink card pushed between the windshield and the wiper blade closest to the driver's side. Distant sound of running water. Mention of a bath. Mention of a place to eat. "Good food at place round corner" etc. The small card is a parking ticket. He opens the door for her. She says thank you. She gets in. He closes the door walks around front of car to other door. He tries to open it but finds it locked. She leans over and pushes up a black plastic peg that locks the car from the inside. Now he can open the door etc. It is possible now to get in etc. Movie end. Title: *Summer Alibi.* He leave cinema alone. She go back study. House very cold. Day called Thursday. The movie ends. Its title: *Panopticon.* She notices that her hands are wet. She dries them on the edge of her jeans. At this point the woman emerges from her bath and commences the ritual of towelling herself dry. She now reaches for a silver object. She is preparing for an evening at the theatre. Room cold. Tape recorder running. Man decides to leave it on and pours himself a drink. Half empty bottle.

Chapter Seventeen of a book entitled *Panopticon* concludes with a sequence of brief utterances issued by the narrator to a nameless party. The latter has entered a study and replaced a book on a shelf. The book is entitled *Summer Alibi.* In the third brief utterance in this sequence the narrator recalls a similar occasion when she too had entered this same room to replace a letter on a rosewood escritoire. Prior to this entry she had bathed in preparation for an evening at the theatre. It is known (from the evidence of a newspaper advertisement described in detail by the narrator) that the title of the play is *The Mark.* Later, in a book entitled *Panopticon,* this same description will reappear. There, however, the play will be a film called *The Mark* and the whole reference will appear as a separate sheet glued over a cancellandum, described by the photographer after printing as resembling a cinematic screen described in a book the same nameless party has written.

Start with the assertion that you never failed to locate the requisite coordinates nor to execute any of the following commands. Let the image of the bath persist and split a second time. Place the woman in the room and in the theatre. This time allow the man to walk away. Follow him until you reach the study door. Don't bother to describe the room, just put him in it. Let him meet the other man. Don't mention names. Allow them to leave the room and walk down into the street where a planned complication will occur. Finish the chapter. Switch off the machine. Now place the pen you'll make him write with equidistant between the two edges of the page where the two men have been left. Add the phrase to your own scenario "she was middle aged." Now mention another room. Let one of the men go into it. Describe his hands. Describe specifically what the hands are doing. Let the two men walk a block or two before you stop them. Watch them carefully. When you bring them back to the study door make sure the door opens inwards (i.e. away from you) and that the hinged side has a long cracked edge. Now watch how he wipes his hands. Memorize where he puts the book. Note the shelf and the adjacent titles. Note the way he dries his hands and how he refolds the towel. Make sure he notices the cracked edge of the door. Force his eyes to follow the wall until they reach the place where you stand. Don't let him see you. Move away at this point and start to type again. Describe his nose. Describe the pair of marks on his left cheek. Make sure there's a new mirror in the bathroom. Make sure you delay him and bring him to the spot too late. Get him anxious. Leave him irritated. Make sure the coffee's cold. Change the time. Set the action in a new place. Change the title. Change the focus of the lens. Turn the lights up to their brightest and shine them directly in his eyes. Repeat the phrase NOTHING NEW WILL OCCUR. Pull back his head by his hair. Keep the curtains closed. Show him the knife. Remove the coffee. Don't let him smoke. Make sure the cup gets broken and that all the coffee spills on the floor. Don't mention the time. Answer all his questions. Bring in a new cup. Now describe the room. Insert four new chairs in the scene you describe. Now change the title to *Toallitas*. Say it's a film being shot in Spain. Tell him that you have a part in it. Tell him it's about a murder on board a boat then leave him alone in the room. Leave him wondering. Leave the lights on bright. Don't take your eyes off him for a second. Change the title again back to *The Mind of Pauline Brain* then move the scene to a different place. Don't let him see where he's going. Place him on a bench in an open park at the east side of the city. Tell him it's spring that he's been very sick and in a coma but that he's now recovering. Now switch on the machine and record everything that follows. Use your own voice. Describe the ducks on the pond in the park. Tell him he's going to be all right. Describe the bench he's sitting on. Mention the plaque on it. Mention the words carved into it and mention the trash can to the side. Don't forget to reassure him in his blindness. Now remain silent. Leave quietly. Don't let him suspect that you're gone. Go back to the study and watch the other man you ordered to write. Ask him all the questions you can think of that might relate to his movements over the past five days. Sit him in a chair with a high back. Focus the bright light on his eyes. Let him finish the sentence he's writing then make him move to the door. Tell him to come back and force him to take up the pen and write some more. Tell the other man that he's being described. If he tries to shift the scene or mentions the strategic sections of the woman emerging from her bath delete him from your own story. Describe him in such a way that he'll appear to be dead. Put parentheses around the whole incident and leave quietly. Replace the entire paragraph with the phrase HIS BODY REMAINED MOTIONLESS AND A COLD LUMP CAME IN HER THROAT. If he writes the words "he's dead" shift your own plot to the scene in the garden and replace the former line with the phrase HE'S MOVING QUIETLY TOWARDS THE GATE. Now you can drop the deceit but don't tell either of them about the contents of the letter. Finish off the interview with a brief history of the place. Polish off the room in a brief sentence. Describe the woman getting out of the bath. Change the title of the book from *The Mind of Pauline Brain* to *Summer Alibi.* Now watch carefully how the keys drop to his feet between his shoes. Don't describe them instead look very carefully at his face. Now watch him pick up the keys. Make him put them on the escritoire. Now make him take them away. Introduce a sudden noise that frightens him. Let him run to the door but make sure the door's locked. Tell him a lie. Tell him you've just returned from a visit to a friend. Lie and say you've forgot his name. Don't mention the movie. Stop the sentence just as he's about to leave. Repeat the phrase I BELIEVE THE DOOR IS ALWAYS KEPT LOCKED. At this point the other man might ask you where the keys are. Tell him you've lost them. Make sure you freeze him and describe him in detail (facial features, mannerisms, family background etc.). Describe your own return to the park. Now interrupt as many conversations as you can. Make sure that he's watching you as you watch him. In the book describe him as a woman. It's important to keep control of this surveillance scenario as long as you possibly can. Don't worry that you can't see the consequences, make sure, however, that when you can't see them that somebody else can. Now you can delete all reference to the keys and door. Repeat the phrase NOTHING NEW WILL OCCUR. Now delete the second man. Remove the eighth, the sixteenth and the thirty ninth paragraphs. Return them to their files in the desk. Now take out the index file and check the possible descriptions permitted you. Pause from your typing to look at the man in the park. Switch off the tape recorder. Check that all relevant books are back on the shelf. Now let him close his eyes. Let him get up from the bench and open them again. Let him walk towards you. Switch the scene suddenly to a year ago in the study. Take off the blindfold and make him turn on the switch. Describe him in a position of abject terror. Tell him it's all right. Make him walk across the floor to the window. Describe him looking out. Replace the blindfold as he reaches the final sentence. Describe him as reading rather than writing. Change the final sentence to something else. Make sure you keep it vague and ambiguous. Leave the body in the room. Now describe whatever you want. When you leave the room make sure the machine's switched off, the book's replaced on the shelf, light out and door securely locked. Check your watch as you leave. It should be precisely nine thirty-seven.

It is a rule of the specific game (the one called "the movie" in the book entitled *The Mark*) that a change in character occur only at a point when the feasibility of plot itself seems dead. A woman, for instance, who emerges from a bath to find the hero (not the killer) standing by her with a knife. A photograph of the knife might show blood on the blade. Blood from a raw lamb chop purchased three days ago from a small butcher's shop owned by a distant relative of the nameless woman. In Chapter Seventeen of a book entitled *Summer Alibi* this shop is described in great detail. Its external features enumerated and the interior rooms and content therein elaborately itemized. It is mentioned too that each day the shop closes at six and is closed all day Sunday. The book describes a hand which, a few seconds before or after six, reaches down to the glass door and reverses a hanging sign. At nine thirty-seven in the morning the sign is turned by the same hand to again read Open. The narrator of *Summer Alibi* imputes great significance to this action and describes an incident of considerable violence occurring one day previously when a woman entered a different shop on the same street to purchase a bottle of shampoo to be used later in her evening shower. The title of the movie in which this entire game scenario is enacted is

The Mind of Pauline Brain. It is understandable how at this point of impasse in both book and movie a certain predictability obtrudes. Once again the camera shows a woman emerging from a bath, towelling herself dry and remembering the incident at the shop. There are red marks on her body to suggest an earlier scenario based on violence. Let us call this last description caused by impasse the "conscious deidealization of the performing properties." The entire movie has now emerged as a misconception, a philosophical mistake on the director's part. The movie is proving to be a major political mistake, the director, a victim (if you like) of a fake historical decision. During actual production many scenes will be cut. It must be imagined that this is how the story of the woman emerging from the bath vanishes. Let us assume that technicians are currently at work trying to retrieve a specific sequence of shots that show a camera held in front of a half concealed rosewood escritoire. The film has apparently snapped causing the loss of a certain number of valuable frames. Hot day. Escritoire bought especially for scene from small antique store in village owned by producer's niece (a part-time writer). Both niece and producer seem embarrassed. She averts face. He put question to her she no mind to answer. Voice at her elbow. The screen becomes blank. In the dark of the theatre only the neon exit signs are perceptible. It is raining outside and the camera focuses upon two solitary people walking down a deserted city street. To their left (but at a distance of several blocks) there is a large illuminated theatre sign. The verbal contents of the sign are in the process of being changed to announce the forthcoming attraction. It is to be a film about analogy and presence, a film based on the game of chess in which all the pieces must be removed from a box in order for a certain biography to continue.

Chapter Twenty Six of a book entitled *The Mind of Pauline Brain* ends with a sequence of brief utterances spoken by the hero to a nameless woman. Previously, the woman has been described as having retired to her bath after a short visit to her study where she replaced a book upon a shelf. The title of this book is *Panopticon*. Previous to this description it was stated that the woman was alone and reading a letter received that morning. During her reading of this letter her mind is described as wandering among a confused memory of the film she had seen three nights ago. The film contains a scene in which a nameless photographer is described as having died. The actual incident is not depicted but through a sequence of brief utterances a strong suggestion is left that the photographer's death was an extremely violent one. The title of the film is *The Mark*. In a brief and critical review of the film published in one of that morning's papers it is mentioned that the film script is based on a book entitled *Summer Alibi* and that in Chapter Thirty Three of that book occurs the incident of a woman reading. It is there that the woman is described as emerging from a bath, towelling herself dry and reaching over to a book upon a shelf. Naked and half dry she reads the spine: *Toallitas*. Despite the title she remembers the book as containing little or no Spanish. She fails to reconstitute the plot except for vague and broken memories with little or no connection. Should these memories themselves be rendered writing they would take the form of a long, extended strip or horizontal band along the bottom of several blank pages. This writing, naturally, she would never find possible to read. It would occur, in effect, as a lineal band of prohibition, a fictive threshold, an exergual space outside her own sphere of existence but within the compass of an authentic reader's eyes.—As if the reader's book alone contained the possibility of that other story. It would be as if the woman had arrived late and in confusion at a cinema, the film already started, the title unknown to her. She sees the image of a man which finally captures her attention. But the screen is entirely vacant. It seems again "as if" the reel of film has snapped and the movie is temporarily interrupted. Whatever the reason when the image finally returns the entire body of the man is no longer in evidence. Now there is the close up of a small hand camera held in front of a face. The image is blurred and granular and might be compared to the stereophonic text of a voice recorded in the worst possible acoustic conditions and in a language the woman cannot understand. To the authentic reader's eyes this might appear as a horizontal band dividing two areas of discourse extended out across the top and bottom of a page. Previous to this band's appearance several pages of texts are presumed to have occurred with no such division. It is assumed the band has snapped and only at this point repaired. Suffice to say that even with the band reconnected there is no point of contact in the several threads of narrative. The film, the book and the tape are said to be hermetic and sealed within the vacuum of a vacant space. There are no proper names to imbricate or link. No reference across the empty spaces. No calling. No touch or utterance. No sudden bump. As such, two people might pass along a street. But there can be no town. No lights. No rooms to occupy. Only two separated and entirely differentiated passages and no specified direction. The possibility of loss has been removed.

And only at this point does she begin to read. She remembers the film has not been processed. The reading continues as though it were a continuous band of sequential inattentions. "For the room is crowded (she is not alone) and the writings of the others make their presence felt as a mixture (*mélange*) of egotism (*egoisme*) and strained feeling (*sensibilité*) along the horizon of the exergue. This speech she hears does not, however, constitute a footnote but what we might call an indifference (*indifférence*)." It is as if a film has already started and she arrives to it late. It is understandable how her reading of the book (its title is *The Mark*) passes by in silence as a band above the band below. Not the footnote. Closer, in fact, to an intercepted wavelength but not of her own interception. Rather a prior interception displacing the speech and rendering it a film, extended, unbroken along the bottom of certain pages. In effect a doubling in which the gap (it is a double gap, a gap both in attention and a gap in sequence) consists of a supposedly "unfinished edge." No point of contact. No reference or cross reference. No calling. Two people passing in a street. No town. No city. No street. Two separate passages. A street. That other street. No lights. No traffic. Two women. A band below them.

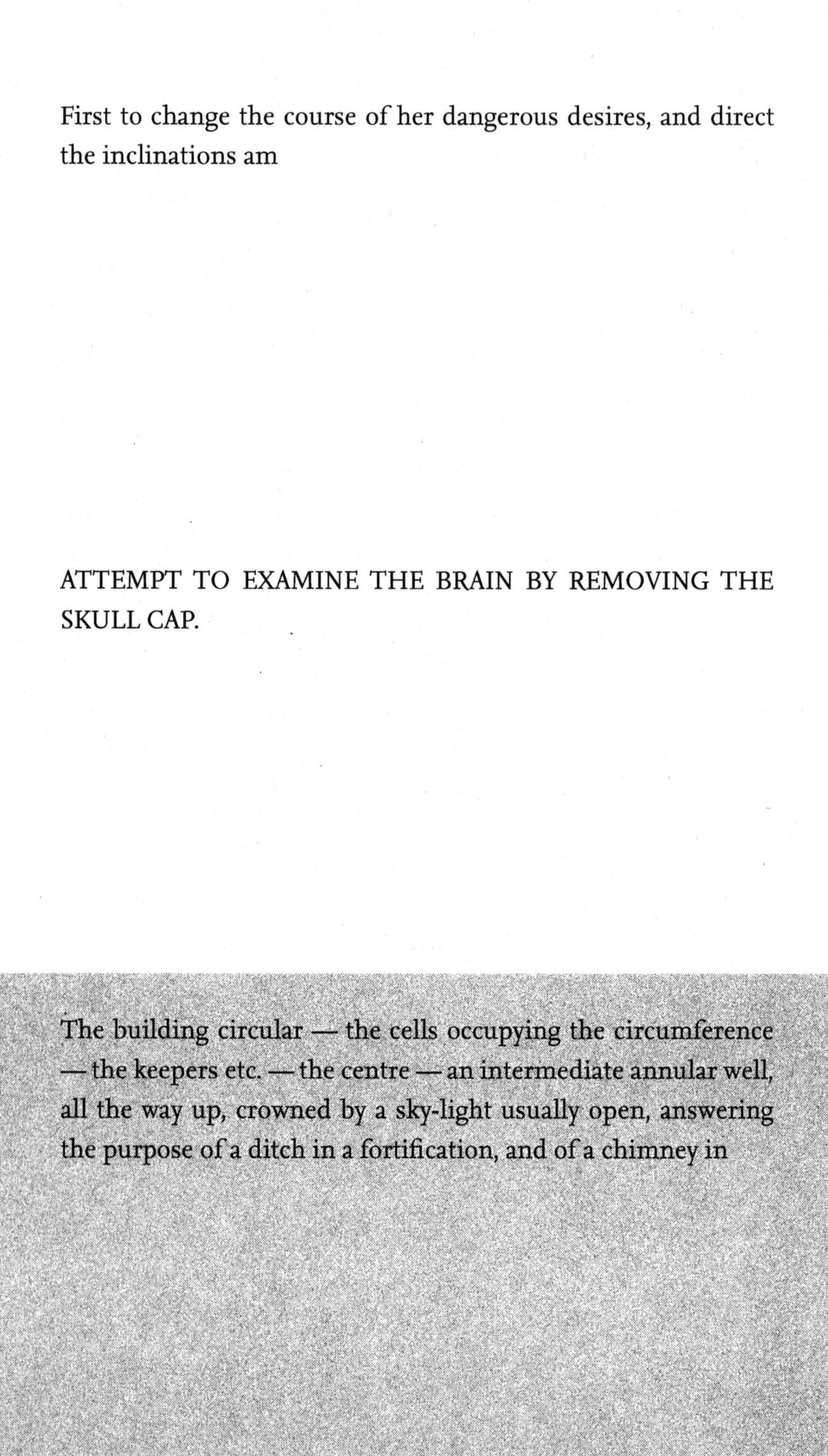

First to change the course of her dangerous desires, and direct the inclinations am

ATTEMPT TO EXAMINE THE BRAIN BY REMOVING THE SKULL CAP.

The building circular — the cells occupying the circumference — the keepers etc. — the centre — an intermediate annular well, all the way up, crowned by a sky-light usually open, answering the purpose of a ditch in a fortification, and of a chimney in

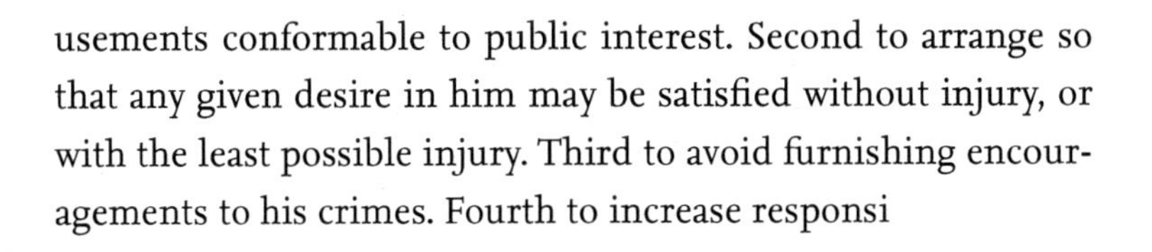

usements conformable to public interest. Second to arrange so that any given desire in him may be satisfied without injury, or with the least possible injury. Third to avoid furnishing encouragements to his crimes. Fourth to increase responsi

YOU MAY DO THIS BY SAWING THROUGH THE EXTERNAL TABLE, THAT IS

ventilation — the cells, laid open to it by an iron grating. The yards without, laid out upon the same principle as also the communication between the building and the yards. The keeper concealed by blinds and other contrivances from the observation of the pri

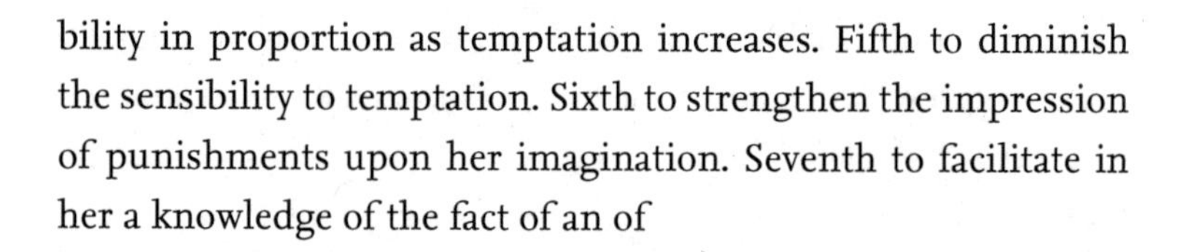

bility in proportion as temptation increases. Fifth to diminish the sensibility to temptation. Sixth to strengthen the impression of punishments upon her imagination. Seventh to facilitate in her a knowledge of the fact of an of

THROUGH THE SECTION COMMENCING IN FRONT AT ABOUT AN INCH ABOVE THE MARGIN OF THE

soner, unless where he thinks fit to show himself: hence, on their part, the sentiment of an invisible omnipresence. The whole circuit reviewable with little, or, if necessary, without any change of place. One station in the inspection part affording the most perfect view of the two stories of cells, and a considerable

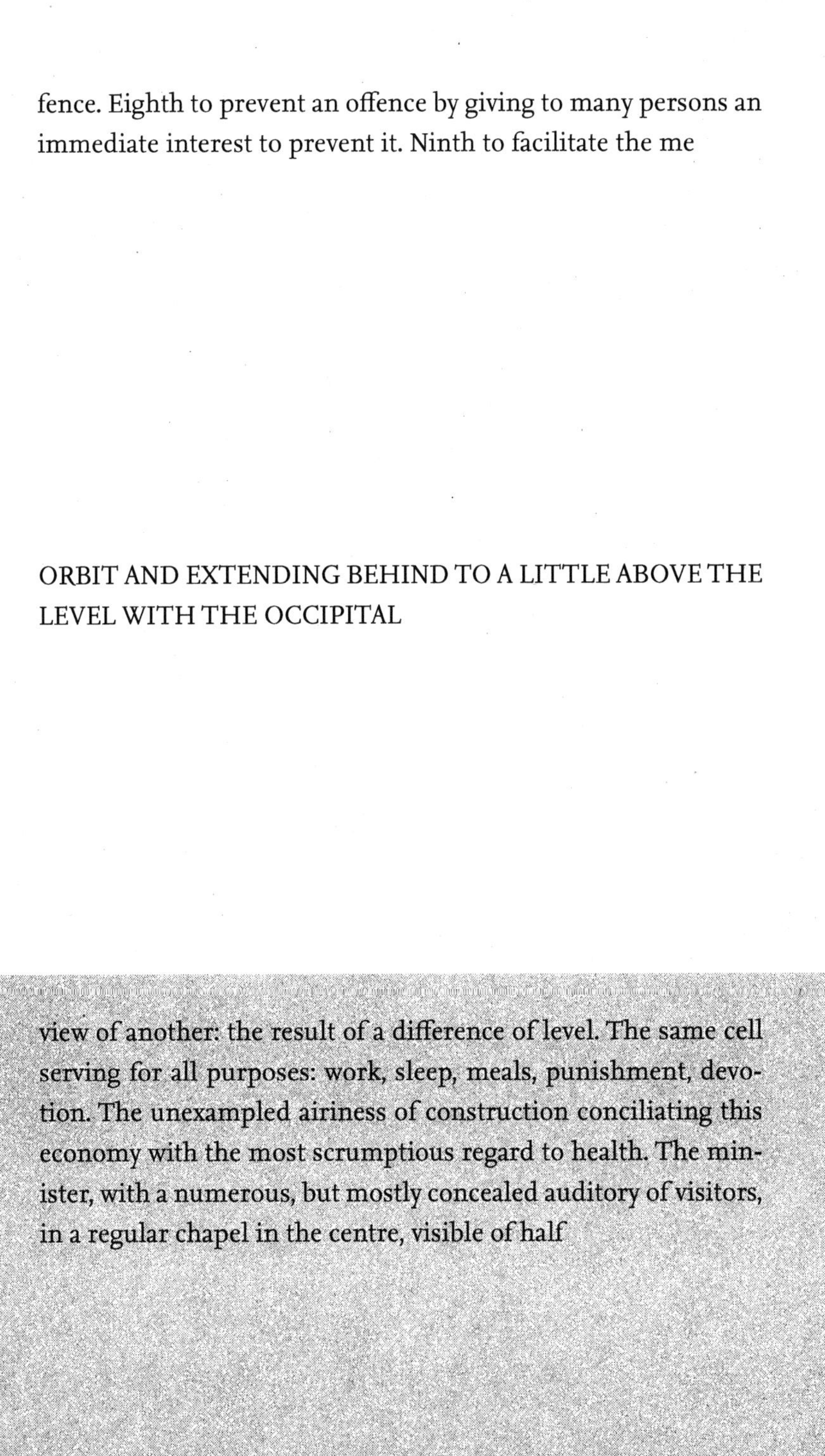

fence. Eighth to prevent an offence by giving to many persons an immediate interest to prevent it. Ninth to facilitate the me

ORBIT AND EXTENDING BEHIND TO A LITTLE ABOVE THE LEVEL WITH THE OCCIPITAL

view of another: the result of a difference of level. The same cell serving for all purposes: work, sleep, meals, punishment, devotion. The unexampled airiness of construction conciliating this economy with the most scrumptious regard to health. The minister, with a numerous, but mostly concealed auditory of visitors, in a regular chapel in the centre, visible of half

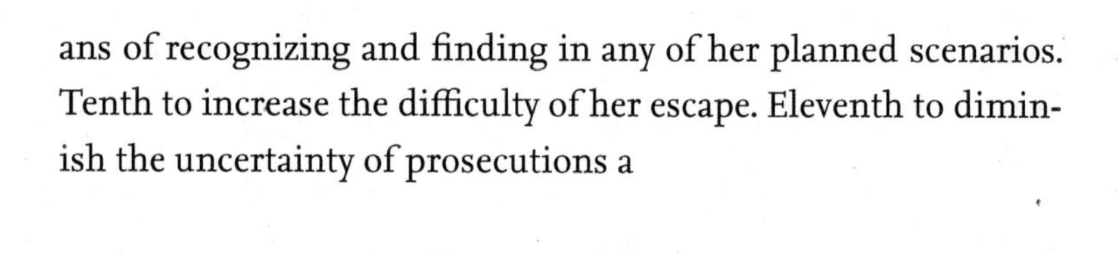
ans of recognizing and finding in any of her planned scenarios. Tenth to increase the difficulty of her escape. Eleventh to diminish the uncertainty of prosecutions a

PROTUBERANCE. THEN BREAK THE INTERNAL TABLE WITH

the cells, which on this occasion may double their complement. The sexes, if both are admitted, invisible to each other. Solitude, or limited seclusions, ad libitum. — But unless for punishment limited seclusion in assorted companies of two, three, and four, is preferred: an arrangement, upon this plan alone exempt from danger. The degree of seclusions fixed upon may be preserved, in

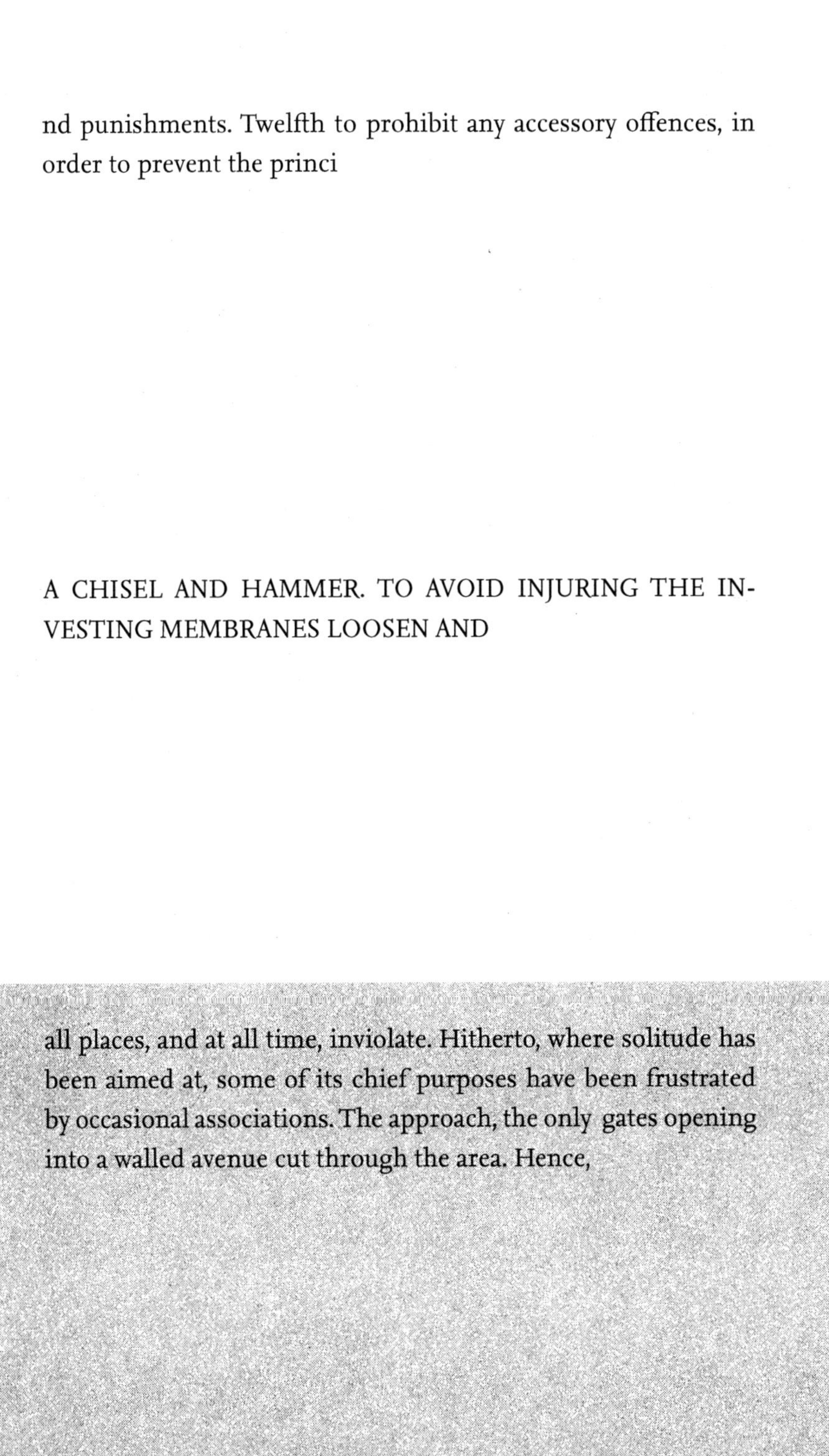
nd punishments. Twelfth to prohibit any accessory offences, in order to prevent the princi

A CHISEL AND HAMMER. TO AVOID INJURING THE INVESTING MEMBRANES LOOSEN AND

all places, and at all time, inviolate. Hitherto, where solitude has been aimed at, some of its chief purposes have been frustrated by occasional associations. The approach, the only gates opening into a walled avenue cut through the area. Hence,

ple offence.

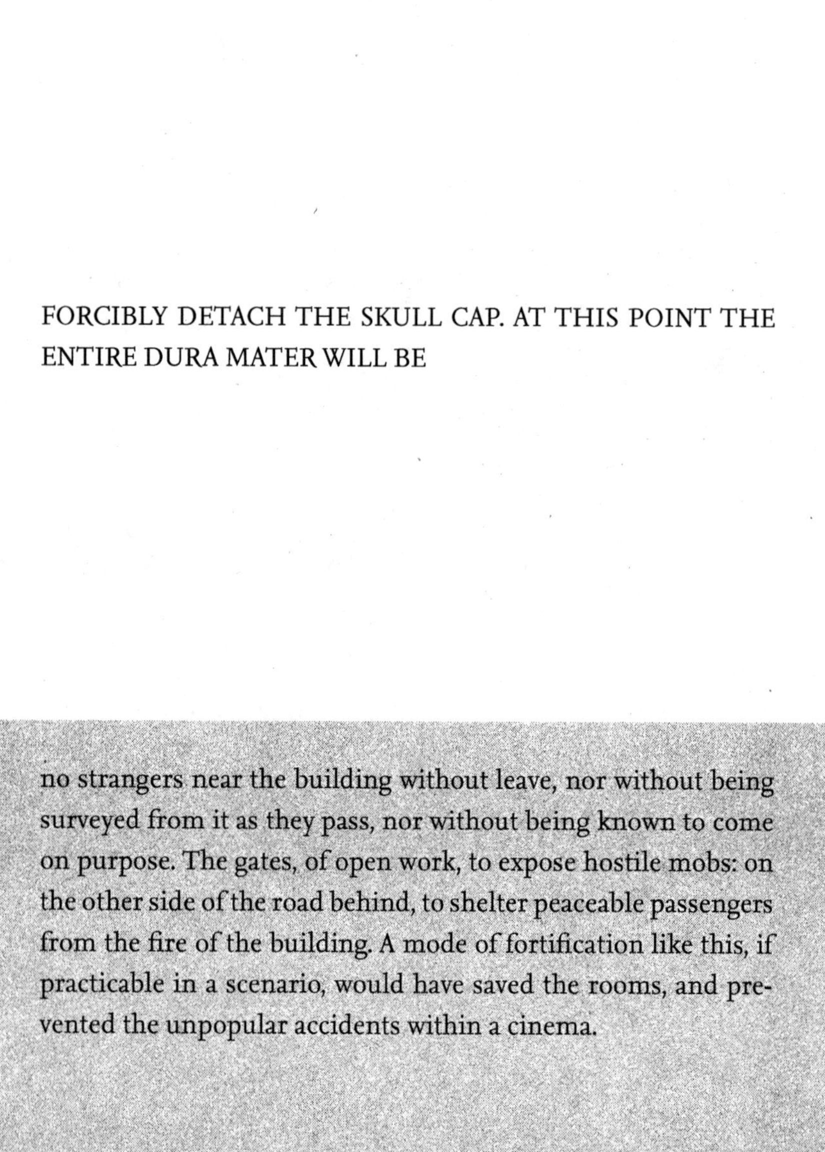

FORCIBLY DETACH THE SKULL CAP. AT THIS POINT THE ENTIRE DURA MATER WILL BE

no strangers near the building without leave, nor without being surveyed from it as they pass, nor without being known to come on purpose. The gates, of open work, to expose hostile mobs: on the other side of the road behind, to shelter peaceable passengers from the fire of the building. A mode of fortification like this, if practicable in a scenario, would have saved the rooms, and prevented the unpopular accidents within a cinema.

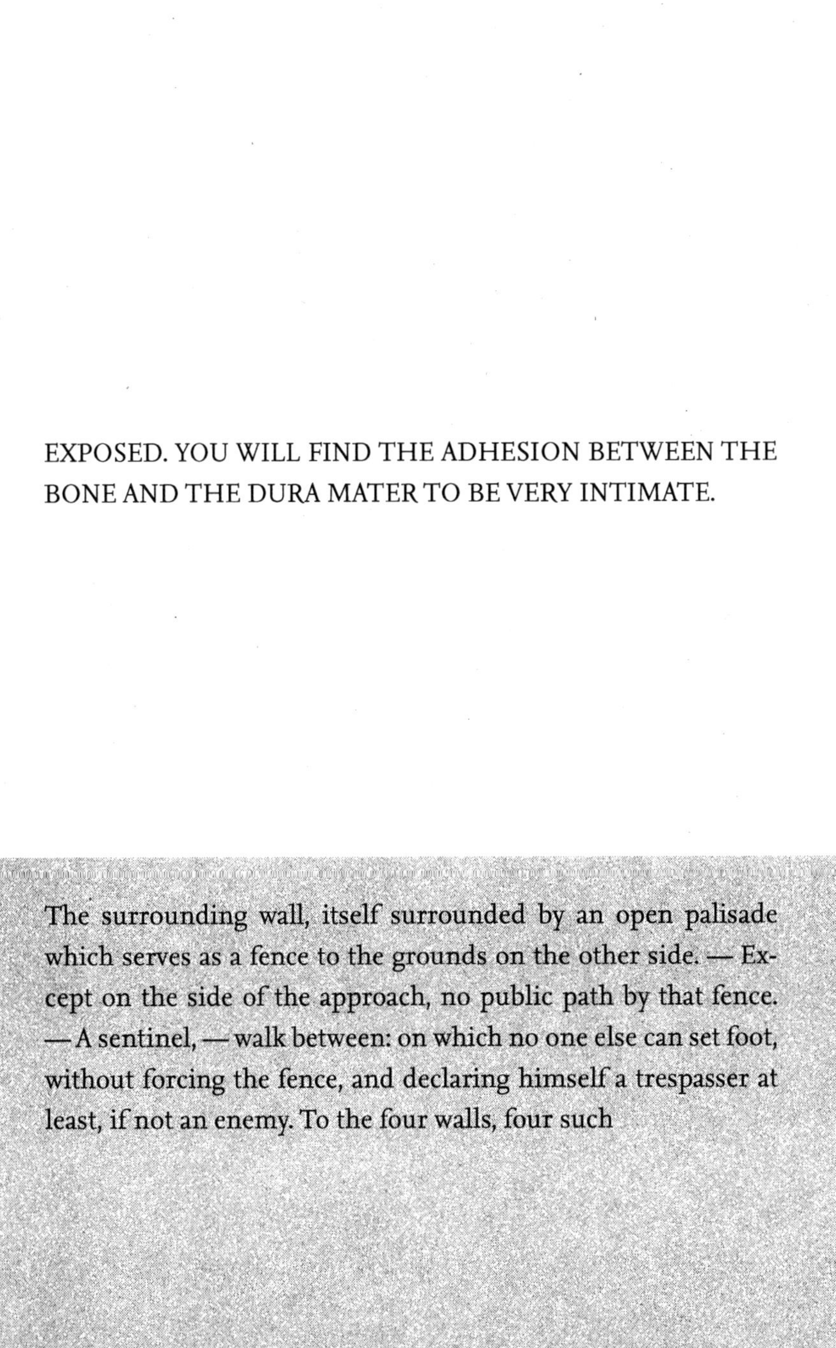

EXPOSED. YOU WILL FIND THE ADHESION BETWEEN THE BONE AND THE DURA MATER TO BE VERY INTIMATE.

The surrounding wall, itself surrounded by an open palisade which serves as a fence to the grounds on the other side. — Except on the side of the approach, no public path by that fence. — A sentinel, — walk between: on which no one else can set foot, without forcing the fence, and declaring himself a trespasser at least, if not an enemy. To the four walls, four such

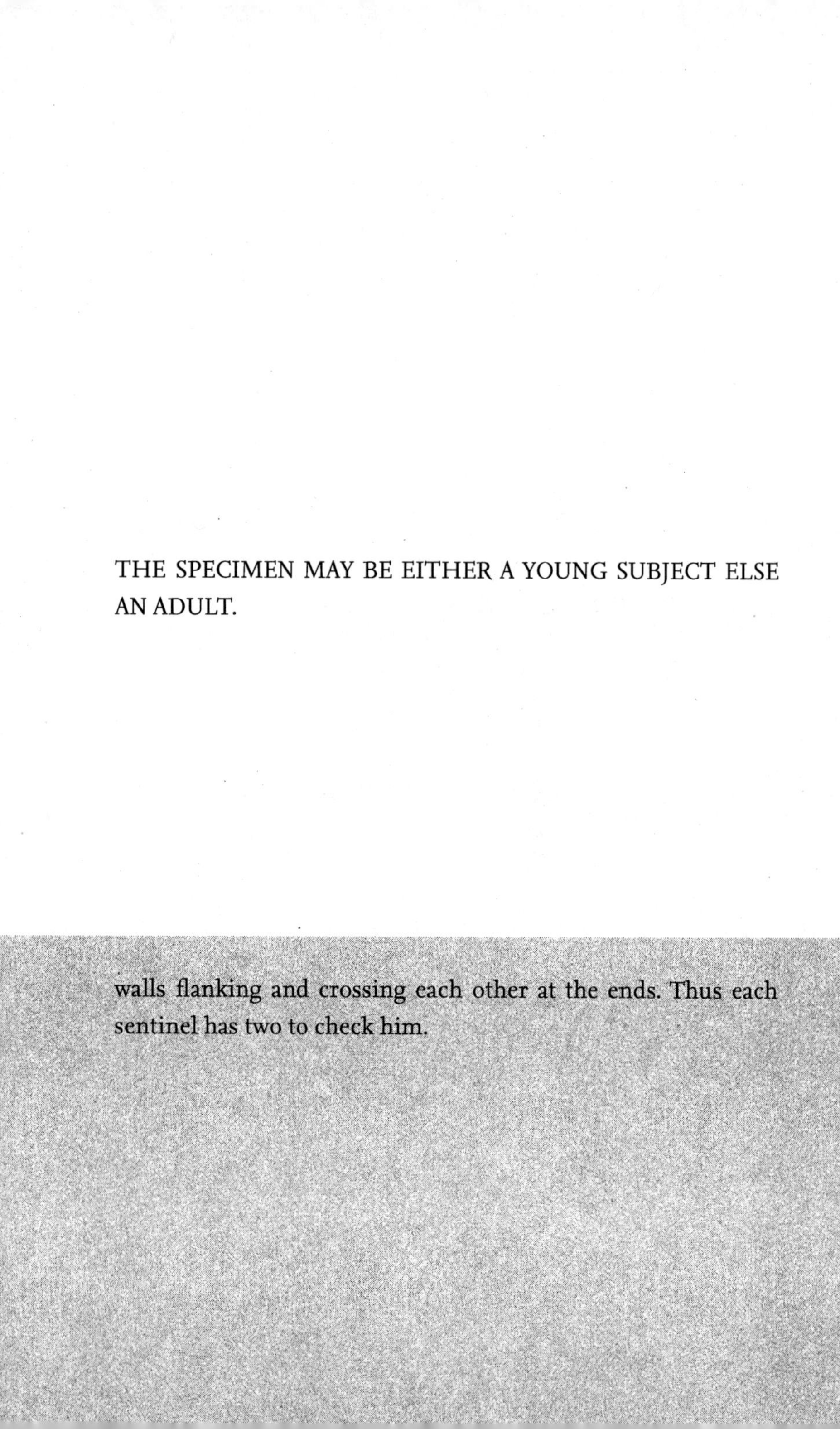

THE SPECIMEN MAY BE EITHER A YOUNG SUBJECT ELSE AN ADULT.

walls flanking and crossing each other at the ends. Thus each sentinel has two to check him.

In order to grasp the full stereophony of the message we must first conceive of them as occupying the separate worlds of DREAM and INTOXICATION. These worlds, like the words that express them, are not far apart. Through practical strivings they flow together into new shapes and partial compounds, both themselves and not themselves, both this man we speak of and this woman he kills. There must be no pleasure in either of these basic actions. To say this is to state the only possible relation between gland and eye, between the entire history of body and tone. It is necessary for all action by both parties to be repeated endlessly and in that way seduced into their broken parts. The victims of dismemberment, pagination, of morselated passages, intersecting shards and planes. The huge dependence of the lungs turned thoraccic, cinematic in a pliant eroticism. In this way only the statements of "pure" language can be understood in the counter-worlds of body and sign. We are envisaging "the condition of the annihilation in relation to that which the earlier meaning of essence dissolved into an empty frame." The camera will follow long after the dogmatism of mere self-certainty has ended. Everything that was purely mediated has, in some way, become unintelligible, violent and opaque. The woman. The bath. The towel. The highly mannered prose of the diary entries. All worn smooth from repetition and hypertrophy. "She" stands in "everybody's" way "primordially" unaffected by any theoretical interpretation. Bad faith is instantaneous and its enjoyment constitutes his universal life therefore he must be shattered into parts. "I must die." For the natural consequences of deeds are no longer natural.

Left Channel: The logic of the body as a mouth.

Right Channel: She spoke only because she found herself within a long tradition of utterance.

The landscape appears as a flat picture, lacking depth structured inside the ontological problematics of this myopia. It has, as it were, passed into philosophy as the daily pleasures of a game of blind man's bluff. Conflict therefore can only manifest as an oscillation between two channels of separate speech, between the zones of a transcendent future (strictly determined) and a system of reference irreducible to the framework of (quote) the woman's instrumental actions (unquote). Should she shower again and emerge from her bath to towel herself dry then the datum of sensation will be co-determined. As the contents of two simultaneous instants of physical time she will pass into being a divided mo(ve)ment of a different consciousness.

On the occasion of the first appearance of the line on the horizon you will begin to construct the machine. On completion you will immediately commence the operation. Ensure that all valves are opened and steam, allowed to flow through the entire engine until the air is completely expelled and then let all the valves be closed. To start the engine let the exhausting valves be opened, the steam will then flow freely

Left Channel: Let us gaze upon the screen in front of us and watch the man as he emerges from his bath reach over for a towel folded on a shelf to commence the ritual of towelling himself dry. Imagine him to be glandular and unitary despite the obvious broken appearance of his parts from which sum emerges a tiny iridescent insect at the service of no one and armed with a terrible discharge. Its beauty is undeniable but let's suppose the lie that its compound eyes are actually a horrid lupin yellow. It is described in detail on a page of Chapter Seven of the book entitled *The Mind of Pauline Brain* as emitting a poisonous gas from its abdomen in the direction of a nameless photographer. At this point, on the screen, this image disappears in a thick pall of smoke. A voice tells us (we assume it's the voice of the hero's lawyer, but it's actually the killer's) that the creature is dividing into twelve separate bodies, not clones, but violent antagonistic rivals. There are painted butterflies upon their gas masks as they walk in a *fylkingen* towards the library.

Right Channel: She is ready and armed for the towering spiral of power and pleasure as the hero moves to avoid her first description. She traps him beneath the folds of her prehistoric cotton,

from the boiler and press upon the lesser piston, and at the same time the steam below the greater piston will flow into the condenser leaving a vacuum in, the greater cylinder. The centre of the great working beam carries the two arch-heads with their enantiomorphic faces on which the chains of the piston rods play. The distance of these arch-heads (the lovers' glands in the earlier draft) from the centre must be in the same proportion as the beneath the stained dress of her deaths. At this point you must imagine a tiny droplet of transparent liquid issue from a duct sequestered in the complex working of a huge machine. The drip is to be pictured falling in slow motion into a small rectangle marked out in yellow chalk upon an empty section of a car park.

Left Channel: She has now removed the yellow powder from her pouch, has spread her six legs and allowed him to inseminate.

Right Channel: At this moment (the moment the insect's left mandible touches the towel) a yellow liquid enters its eyes.

length of the cylinders in order that the same play of the beam may correspond to the play of both pistons. The screen shows a tube by which communication may be opened by way of the valve located between the top and the bottom of the lesser maternal cylinder, the top of the greater paternal cylinder and the filial tube that leads to the condenser by way of the exhausting valve. The auditorium is silent. As the pistons descend the steam

She confessed to just a single deletion, an incident in Chapter Eighteen of a book called *The Mark* involving fellatio with the body of the woman's former lover. "i dreamt i was a machine, that i was called his belt loom. Seven hundred lines of weft like single bands of text intersect my warp within the regular alternation of the stitches. i dreamt there was a place for me within the unwritten history of this fabric. My maiden shawl is what i wear it is made from the memories of former loves. It's not a mythology. But it's not a truth. Yet it can't be excluded. The entire operation seemed silly. The yarn was tied to one end of his arm stump then strung from his balls in a series of concentric figures over the fingers of the right hand until the required width of warp was obtained."

"The dead men are all called shreds."

Right Channel: Everything is said now about the last two years. They hated circularity. The sentences repositioned out of reach, out of fear and lust, in a diary entry: "Thursday and over the hill

which is between them is constantly increasing in its bulk and therefore descending by a greater pressure ... there is scattered laughter at this point ... then the camera angle changes to emphasize the disconnection from the sound track ... the valves are now worked by the engine itself, both the woman and the nameless photographer scream by means similar to those already described ... heads of boilers are flat and burning hot ... tubes are there must be another landscape."

Left Channel: ... subauditions of these illittrefactions ... but where ... you don't know a thing. The rest indistinguishable.

Right Channel: If the woman can be described and named she will become all echo. In that way the man alone will be saved by facts. All the rest is about how the children will hate you. Letting you live. You're welcome. *Left Channel:* If this is the body we shall kill it. *Right Channel:* To stand exposed to a death is to stand reinstituted as a temporal unit of enduring property. *Left Channel:* A phenomenon, then, can be no "substantial" unity. *Right Channel:* Substantial, no. The phenomenon has no authentic properties and knows no real changes, no real parts and no causality. *Left Channel:* So let the others come and find their own death in description. *Right Channel:* Description yes, but we must assume a reason for every event. We must insist that every act occurs because it is willed or wanted. Which is to say ... *Left Channel:* There can be no language at the service of nothing. *Right Channel:* (Silent) ...

reinserted ... voice over screaming continues ... laughter terminates.

Left Channel: And it is across such a distance that desire itself desires.

Right Channel: Where is the moon.
Left Channel: A person killed it.

Right Channel: Where is the name of the sun.

Left Channel: If the steam gauge is used as a measure of the strength of the steam which presses on the piston, it ought to be on the same side of the throttle valve as the cylinder; for if it were on the same side of the throttle valve with the boiler, it would not be affected by the changes which the steam may undergo in passing through the throttle valve, when partially closed by the agency of the governor. Chapter Seven mentions how the hero uses a

Photon: noun or any of its parts.

The parts he placed in his phylactery. Apposite phobia for milk. The passage of words see: succession, see: substitutive. Her role in substitutes, see: specific place meant, see: repetition of the phrase "there still is a use to holding mirrors." The landscape intensely itemized, see: window, verb: to look through as if beyond to some forbidden place, see: taboo, see: replacement of the voice with written message, see: reference, see: repetition of the word "paraphrase" (as in "you both seem tired today.") see: at my wit's end, see: limit &/or threshold, as in "edge" or border, see: a very thin edge as on a board or tool, see: instrument ... "and

slightly inclined grate at the back of the lower end of that which remains of the common genitalia and at the front, or upper end, the hopper for admitting coals. In the bottom or narrow end of the hopper is a moveable sheath that conceals the tool. It is described how, on drawing back this sheath, a small quantity of fuel was allowed to descend upon a fixed shelf under the hopper. It is mentioned too how when the shelf returns the fuel is protruded the lake in front of us through all of this at once a machination and a coda," or cog, see: blunt bow or stern (it was her memory of lakes we sought to remove, compare: "evanishment," compare: "the cottage by the sea, the chalk cliffs, the talk of poisonous roots in some of the plants") see: colchium, compare: efficient sub-plot, see: place of death as in "to take place," as in a reference to wedding, dying, murder, suspect "all the legends of this area" (see: calendar, chronosology, see: "an entire sheet of flame," see: cosmogony ..."the gods set as teeth around the rim of a wheel"; see: transportation; compare: this sentence transports us" ... a progression ... the line, see: caravan not carapace, see: "blend" "blanch" and "bleeding heart" ... "the reference here is to the sphalerite not the sphere," see: blind-fish fixed at a distance, see: "suck" alternative go down on, comparison with "decomposition made the body attractive," repetition of the theme "going down on the dead," see: necrophilia, compare: the proposed limits of transgression, as in "the histrionics of its fancy," as in "a knock," "a double bump," compare: "hit" in action, in the sentence "the car hit the tree at a terrible speed," compare theme of death, see: "hit" in the sentence "she hit him hard across the face with a terrible blow," repetition of the phrase: "the impact proved fatal,"

forward upon the grate. *Right Channel:* Every alternate bar of the grate is fixed to prevent escape, but the intermediate ones are connected with levers by which they are moved alternately up and down ... (mild laughter at this point) ... The effect is that the coals upon the bar are constantly stirred and gradually advanced by their own force of desire from the front of the grate, where they fall from the hopper to their climacteric. *Left Channel:* By the compare: foetal as in "the foetal damage was most disconcerting," see: "no remains were found, but the difficult heterogeneity of the fragments made coming back to life impossible," see: pronoun, see: "collection," compare: discharge and "dispersal as of seed" ... "and they claimed that they actually heard the lungs pop and saw one eye fall out into a saucer," cross-reference this to "method" and "intent," delete: "those other humilities she termed movement, speech (locution), termination, sequence, circularity," reinstate: "locution," add the phrase: "the meeting place was very hard to find."

shape and construction of the bars, the air is conducted upwards between them and rushes through the burning sperm so as to activate the entire surface of the screen. *Right Channel:* It is an insect. *Left Channel:* It is alive. The screen now presents itself as an entire sheet of flame. *Voice-over:* We must imagine this machine at the service of nobody, a machine without a head, without a base. The pistons incompatible yet mutually desiring. Heat is the principle

A woman arriving at a door (in a movie called *Summer Alibi*) is shown in the process of commencing the operation of opening a study door. Her right hand is described as being motionless at the precise moment it makes contact with a white porcelain handle. Six pages later she is described as entering a bathtub. Her legs are described as "scarred" and "swollen"; her left eye as discharging a yellow coloured mucus. It has been decided that the time will be the fall. A chilly morning plus parasites. A hidden transcript. A lost letter. A sound-track running backwards. It is a very ordinary soot. They say there were no suggestions pointing to a struggle. A hint of cloud. They say that the hinterland is

of its existence and its extinction. The boiler (heart) acts the part of the heart (boiler) from which the vivifying fluid rushes copiously through all its tubes (meandering speakers) where, having discharged (the various functions of life) and deposited its heat (cogitation) in the proper place (the requisite celibate domain), it returns again to its source to be duly prepared for another circulation. *Left Channel:* The mirrors let me look and see that I'm always the district behind a coast and a river. Is mother dead. Do you like lettuce. Are there two kinds of colchium in the garden. A hip is also an exclamation mark used in cheers. What reader doesn't know that empty glasses are sometimes found in hippodromes. This simple statement contains the entire principle of the plot, see: pivot, compare: hinge. If you smell a bit hircine then you must be like a goat. Who said that to whom. It was very damp where the body was found. Why has the door been closed. Whose eyes are those opening. The final days were especially hot. Where are your socks my dear. You can take hold of the toes and break the bones so they can all fold up like pages. Isn't that cute. Daddy didn't hear the noise upstairs i made and when "she" returns from breakfast then "the telephone" will occur. So when i screamed she screamed as well. You drop everything in the dark by the bell on the stairway.

not the one involved, that the pronoun reflected isn't me. *Right Channel:* The mirrors allow me to transform with no external assistance. As a structural being there is nothing human breathing, nothing human oscillating, just the regular anacoluthonic patterns and frictions of an insect mating. *Voice-over:* Let us imagine this language at the service of nobody and the purpose of each sentence to match symmetrically the purpose of death in all the

LEFT CHANNEL: *transcendent. future. aufhebung. strict determination. time. plot. character. discourse critical. nosological. imagination.*

RIGHT CHANNEL: *dialogic. system of reference irreducible to framework of the woman's instrumental actions. suppression of desire. circulation of libido. flux. force. fellatio.*

STEREOPHONIC REALIZATION: You take all the toes and break the bones so they can all fold up. This is a table. Put things on it. Put objects in position. Set a scene. Where are your socks. Your bedroom door it has slammed. The window why opening. When they all return from breakfast the telephone "may and may not" occur.

former drafts. Irrelevant and parasitic on these faces that you see upon this screen. The woman you watch bathing watching you as you yourself are towelled dry ... (at this point the title *Toallitas* flashes on the screen over the image of the same woman typing) ... indifferent vocabulary through the compound mouths of all these cybernetic selves ... discharged into the very heart of the somnambulistic machinery. There is coughing throughout

LEFT CHANNEL:

Organism in its irresistible tabloid of movement. Backwards then forwards moving the body to one side, toes bound tightly, raw material the glands without the body. Didn't you hear that toe snap. Didn't I tell you the window wouldn't close. Doesn't your right eye unzip. Seven further instances (compare "example" in the repetition "example constitutes the major part of disappearance."

RIGHT CHANNEL:

We discover then, in the stated actions of others the origin of plot, pronoun, character and corpse. It institutes the history of an amniotic error. In a sense the female form itself. Which is the glands. Which constitutes the hair. You want to perfect woman and you get her and you tear her to pieces. Whose fault is that. As the story goes, now there's plot to tell it, it must be the killing of a death already perpetrated, but never realized when finalized in words.

the auditorium. The hero moves towards the door. Repetition of the phrase orthodox androgynous superimposition. Repetition of the image: parasite. First occurrence of the phrase "surplus discharge." On the screen they are describing certain images falling into contradiction. But now, to the sound of heavy breathing from behind both their backs, they sit silent meditating on a phrase repeated endlessly.

RIGHT CHANNEL:

We discover then no message. Just an ultimate effect of the mandible that holds the written core of wrist coordinate with sound and sign assuring its body of an infinite horizon.

798: Between imagination and fellatio falls the intellect which would divide. Very real very chilling very close to a risible death cut out beyond happening beyond occurrence closer than near is to your own primordial vocabulary. 799:

PLATES 85–93

Pure thought. In its own delay. Alleged dehiscence. Actions said to occur within any division. Any sense. Any value. A sample of plot might demonstrate. Left Channel: A man returns from a visit to a cinema, enters his apartment by a rear door, undresses and takes a bath. Right Channel: A woman turns the pages of a book from page 165 to page 166. Left Channel: Page 189: a woman emerges from a bath into the pleasure of reputation, repetition, infamous imposture etc. Right Channel: Page 203: description of a hand depositing a cigarette inside a green jade ashtray. Description of the same hand moving over the surface of a rosewood escritoire to object number seven viz. a small portable cassette tape recorder.

Writing and dying. Writing it all down in order to kill. Writing the verb. Across a distance. The body as interrogation. The body as threshold.

Finality: Problematic gland. The body as threat. On the edge of a share. The body in place. Cut. The body as fragment. The pornograph. Next of kin. Skin trade. The body as frame as frame-up as the beginning the end the middle continuous etc.

I WILL HOLD YOU BACK I WILL HOLD YOU WITHIN THIS THING I AM YOUR MOTHER YOU ARE MY CHILD IT IS SIMPLY THE WAY IT IS IT HAS TO BE IT CANNOT BE OTHER THAN THIS LOOK I HOLD UP A SIGN THAT TELLS YOU CERTAIN OLD NAMES HAUNT YOU FIX YOU IN POSITION PLACED TO REPLACE YOURSELF AS MY CHILD AND MY CHILD ALONE THROUGH MY VOICE THROUGH MY EYES POSSESSED ENCRYPTED SO MUCH THAT YOU PARTAKE OF ME ASSUME MY HAZE ARRIVE IN MY PRESENCE DEFERRED IN THE FRAGILE WORDS YOU WILL WRITE WHICH CANNOT BE WHERE I AM WHERE YOU WANT TO BE AND SPEAKING MY WORDS YOU WILL TELL ME YOU LOVE ME AND FORGIVE ME FOR ERASING YOU MAKING YOU A WOMAN PLACED IN QUOTATIONS BY A HAND LIKE A HOOK LIKE THE STITCHES OF A WOUND MADE VOICE TO MAKE ME UP A BODY OUT OF PARTS OUT OF GLANDS TO MAKE MURDER PLEASANT MERELY PHILOSOPHICAL. IT IS THE FATE OF WRITING TO BECOME A STATUE. THERE IS NO OTHER NEED FOR ETC. REVOLUTION THE BODY'S OLD TRADITION WHICH YOU ETC. ALREADY ANNOUNCING YOU A DIFFERENCE THAN PERSON. I WILL LINK ALL CONSIDER-

The body as a woman or a man emerging from a bath or from the sea. The body disjunctive, You see a face, a surface. You hear the surf. You seem to feel the face splash the surf on the surface of. The body for sure. You suppose the skin to sink. You suppose the ink starts to cut it. The body as skin the body between inks expanding a narrative a story.

ATION TO THIS NAME AND SOONER THAN THIS ETC. IT IS STILL NECESSARY AND ETC. YOU ANNOUNCE YOURSELF TO THE MAN IN THE MOVIE AS A SET OF POSSIBILITIES FRAMED AS A WOMAN IN EMERGENCE FROM A BATH OF HUMAN FACTS THE FACE THE HIPS THE TITS THE CROTCH THE HANDS ETC. THE POSSIBILITY FOR ECHO FOR UNDERSTANDING SPEED AS DISTRIBUTION OF A SECOND CHARACTER EMERGING FROM A PARASITIC SHOWER LINEAR INHERITED AND SUBTERFUGE. THE POSSIBILITY OF MURDER OF DESCRIPTION OF THE HUMAN FACT. POSSIBILITIES OF NOTORIOUS CUTS AND GEOGRAPHIC SEGMENTS HOW TO PLACE YOURSELF BESIDE IN FRONT DESPITE OF HER ETC. POSSIBILITIES FOR A CARING LESS FOR WISDOM ACQUIRED THROUGH THE TRUTHS PORNOGRAPHIES AFFORD THAN FOR THE FUTILE AXIOMS OF YOUR DITCHED INTELLIGENCE. I AM YOUR MOTHER. I AM OPENING YOUR FILE. I AM DETERMINED TO CHANGE THE COURSE OF YOUR DANGEROUS DESIRES. WHETHER I AM TRUTH OR AWAKE IS UP TO YOU.

The movie shown in a cinema of an event or a picture or a dream a memory etc. The features of a writer's face. The body as location. A surface. Her skin. Her inks. His "I imagine she imagines insects." The body as photograph the body in light the writing lost in light. The body by definition. The cutting that is the body as elision. The body as deletion. Cut to a woman's room ... the body ... as command ... cut ... to photograph (or instant? or failure? or hope that? for? between? etc.?) The body

LEFT CHANNEL: These are the limits of the edit of the cut of the grafting I onto the eye no ear to weave to interweave intervene entertain ask how certain of the conditions are fulfilled not fulfilled but upheld by a hand on a camera by a hand in function by a sign the hand makes as it drives the great machine as she leaves for the umpteenth time leaving coins on a table for the waiter who brought the wine.

as camera as gun as the words sound in a blinding light. The story of the body of a lady. The body in a story called The Mark *in the film called* Toallitas. *The body which vanishes. The body as effect as removal as displacement. Overloaded plot with light.*

LEFT CHANNEL:

a photograph. a photograph of a paragraph. a paragraph about photography. whose photography. the man's photography. the photography of every seen thing. which things. things the photographer sees. the photographer in the paragraph.

the phrase repeated inside of a description. the phrase no one can remember. a paragraph about forgetting an action. which paragraph. the one the woman remembers. the action the photographer does.

memories of writing. memories of writing this down. memo-

THIRD SCREEN:

a picture. the description of a picture. the picture of a place and the description of an action. what action. the action of bathing. the description of a woman taking a bath. which bath. the bath the photographer sees. which photographer. the one in the photograph.

all about reading. all about written things. the things the woman forgot to write about. a picture of a woman in a bath.

something about remembering an action in a place. which place. the place you look at. the place I'm pointing to and hop-

The body as identity. I have listened with a certain interest. I have turned the page. Page 7: "beginning to smile." Page 65: "town epoch dress nation situation friendship threat etc." The body as page. I have turned a page and reached a surface. Page 34: "A sheet." Page 492: A sheath." The body as mouth. There was a beginning to it all.

ries of the words placed wrong. which words. any words. the words about the photographer.

the description of a blue sky. a paragraph about photography in a clear light.

the mention of a book.

RIGHT CHANNEL:

a photographer in a paragraph. the man in the photograph who looks at you. the man with a camera who the other woman describes.

LEFT CHANNEL:

something about description. ing you look. hoping you see again. hoping you describe.

the mention of a lens. the lens you focus on a woman. which woman. the woman in the photograph. which photograph. the one mentioned in the paragraph.

FIRST SCREEN:

the man you see through a window in a room the man with a pen in his hand that the woman sees.

the woman who simply looks. the woman who doesn't write. something about reading. something about words on a

A myth of origin in a book. Knot the page. Not a plot. To have woven stories. The body as confession. "No stories." Deleted. "Never again." Deleted. Description. The body as waves. Death drives. e.g. "they were both killed in a car crash." The body as friend. Compare "having reached the face." Both channels: "I took a bath." Both screens: (The same image, a different locale, a lady, the hero, the killer's lawyer.)

something about seeing with a gun. which gun. the gun in the book the woman reads.

all about reading. all about the story of the body of a woman or a man. all about identity and place.

something about finding and losing yourself. writing about photography. taking a photo of a book. which book. the book about the different ways of seeing things. things you see not things you listen to.

how does it end. you remember the man in the photograph. the man forgetting what he does.

paper in sunlight.

the body of a woman on a beach in sunlight.

all about photography. all about writing with light. light the photographer sees. light the woman reads by.
something about ending. something about memorizing a conclusion. something about an ending in a place. a place somewhere on this screen. the place where the woman reappears.

before a window.
in a book. on a shelf.
on a screen.

Alternative take: Place i.e. "where did you take it," (a room in the movie, a small house in the book, the copy of the film in both the book and the movie, the porcelain bath in the book, of metal in the film). Left Channel: Involute. It's a kind of roulette and we can both roll in it. Right Channel: The inability of memory to be anything else but "memory."

the place in the paragraph. the paragraph that describes the place where the lens is. the camera held by the woman. the hand that holds the camera. which camera.

the camera in the book.

RIGHT CHANNEL:

in a story.

identical page.

this is a gun.

someone says don't.

SECOND SCREEN:

another story.

identical lens.

a room in which men walk.

men who talk as they walk.

Left Channel: When i stand alone i enter a long tradition of utterance.

Right Channel: Repetition of the phrase "there can be no movie."

all about defending yourself. something about dying.

nobody does. either nobody can or else nobody wants to.

all about choice.

a pen in a hand.

LEFT CHANNEL:

all about identity. a sun in a lens. a lens focused on an object moving. an object casting shadows over a place. which place. the page in a book where the woman starts writing.

something about confusion in an empty space.

in a box.

a blank space beneath her. an empty frame. a strip of film.

on a page.

Left Channel: Static.

Right Channel: Voice over credits over music.

PLATE 97

“There is a night with a certain light you put me in and so i live my life as if it were the book i will never find it possible to write. This is my story but you write it and that way I alone begin to become. As he kisses me he reads me and the kiss itself doesn’t make it light. Finally someone tells me it’s the night. Soon to be day again the night a distant darkness you cut your fingers on. An unfinished edge on which you’re put. It’s not that I’m really dead but rather described. That’s how all the meanings alter. Millions of things are the same as this.”

PLATES 101–117

Part II

SUMMER ALIBI

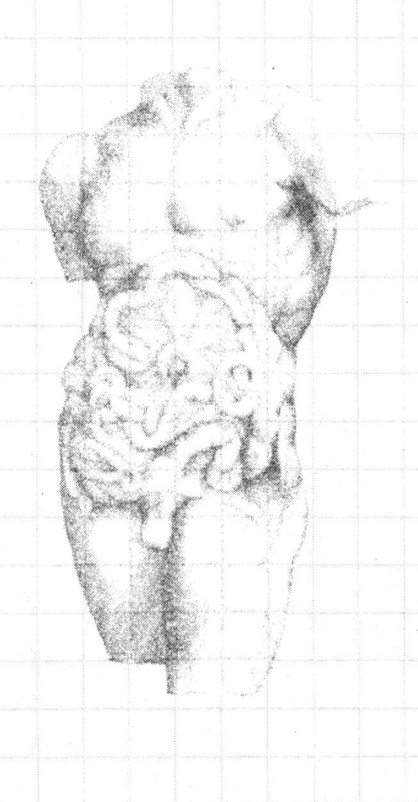

Chapter Seventeen of a book entitled *Panopticon* concludes with a sequence of brief utterances issued by the narrator to a nameless party. The latter has entered a study and replaced a book on a shelf. The book is entitled *Summer Alibi.* In the third brief utterance in this sequence the narrator recalls a similar occasion when she too had entered this same room to replace a letter on a rosewood escritoire. Prior to this entry she had bathed in preparation for an evening at the theatre. It is known (from the evidence of a newspaper advertisement described in detail by the narrator) that the title of the play is *The Mark.* Later, in a book entitled *Panopticon,* this same description will reappear. There, however, the play will be a film called *The Mark* and the whole reference will appear as a separate sheet glued over a cancellandum, described by the photographer after printing as resembling a cinematic screen described in a book the same nameless party has written.

The illustrations described in detail by the narrator demonstrate the final stage in the order of dissection with little more than the naked skeleton left. On the table, beside the book, is a small flask of glue, a pair of scissors and a rule.

At this point there is a rule expressly forbidding further description. The narrative voice is replaced by a small portable cassette tape recorder the magnetic tape within which contains seven minutes thirty-two seconds of discourse. There is an additional command that this machine only be played at night in total silence and dark.

THE TEXTUAL INTENTION PRESUPPOSES READERS WHO KNOW THE LANGUAGE CONSPIRACY IN OPERATION. THE MARK IS NOT IN-ITSELF BUT IN RELATION-TO OTHER MARKS. THE MARK SEEKS THE SEEKER OF THE SYSTEM BEHIND THE EVENTS. THE MARK INSCRIBES THE I WHICH IS THE HER IN THE IT WHICH MEANING MOVES THROUGH. A TEXTUAL SYSTEM UNDERLIES EVERY TEXTUAL EVENT THAT CONSTITUTES "THIS STORY" HOWEVER THE TEXTUAL HERMENEUSIS OF "THIS STORY" DOES NOT NECESSARILY COMPRISE A TOTAL TEXTUAL READING. THE TELEOLOGY OF "THIS MARK BEFORE YOU" DOES NOT SIGNIFY PER SE BUT RATHER MOVES TOWARDS A SIGNIFICATION. HENCE THE MOST IMPORTANT FEATURE OF "THIS MARK" IS NOT ITS MEANING BUT THE WAY IN WHICH "THAT MEANING" IS PRODUCED. ACCORDINGLY THE MARK FOCUSES UPON THE HOW-NESS RATHER THAN THE WHAT-NESS OF MEANING. THIS STORY IS NOT A TEXT IT IS NOT WRITTEN TO MANIFEST SUCH A MOVEMENT OF SIGNIFICATION EVEN THOUGH SUCH A MANIFESTATION IS EFFECTED IN ORDER TO HUMANIZE THE SIGN. HENCE IT IS A LIE THAT THIS STORY IS NOT A TEXT WRITTEN TO MANIFEST SUCH A MOVEMENT BECAUSE THE TEXT BEFORE US IS DISTINCT AND MANIFESTS ITS DISTINCTION. IT IS THE DISTINCTION PER SE THAT IS IMPORTANT NOT THE CONTENT OF THIS DISTINCTION. THE POTENTIAL MEANING OF THE MARK INCREASES WITH THE PROLIFERATION OF EACH OF THE EMPTY DISTINCTIONS. THAT SEX IS NOT A LANGUAGE BUT A LITERATURE. THAT WE SPEAK IN ORDER TO DESTROY THE AURA OF LISTENING. THAT THE MARK UNDERMINES THE MEANING IT ELABORATES.

THAT THE MARK PROVIDES AN ANSWER TO A QUESTION UNPOSED AND UNPOSSESSIBLE. THAT TEXTUALITY IN FACT BECOMES AN INVERSE CATECHISM HENCE A DESIGN FOR LITOTES. TO EXPLAIN EACH WORD WOULD BE TO ANALYSE ITS PLACEMENT IN A SYSTEM OF SIGNS. REPETITION OF THE PHRASE "THAT WHICH SEGMENTS ALSO CLASSIFIES." REPETITION OF THE PHRASE "WHAT CLASSIFIES MUST ALSO SEGMENT." REPETITION OF THE PHRASE "WE ARE THE SAME THROUGH OUR DIFFERENCES." REPETITION OF THE PHRASE "WHAT STRUCTURALLY OPPOSES ALLUSIVELY REFERS." REPETITION OF THE PROPOSITION "THAT CHARACTER IS NOT ALWAYS THE DETERMINATION OF INCIDENT NOR DOES EVERY NARRATIVE CONSIST OF THE ILLUSTRATION OF CHARACTER." REPETITION OF CONCLUSION THAT CHARACTER MAY OCCUPY AN INDETERMINATE ZONE BETWEEN THE PHRASE "THIS POTENTIAL STORY" AND THE PHRASE "THIS STORY OF A LIFE." WE ARE HENCE IN THE REALM OF STRICTLY NARRATIVE BEINGS HOWEVER MUCH TEXTS SHARE WITH LANGUAGE ITS CONTRADICTORY STRUCTURE. ERADICATION OF ALL PREVIOUS STATEMENTS. SUBSTITUTION OF PHRASE "THE MEANING OF THE MARK RESIDES IN LANGUAGE AS AN INSTITUTION." REPETITION OF SUPPORTING PHRASE "A WRITER IS NOT THE PERSON WHO THINKS IN TEXTS BUT THE PERSON WHO ALL MARKS MOVE TO THINK THEMSELVES INSIDE HIM." FINAL REPETITION OF CORRECTION: "FOR HIM READ HER."

PINPRICKS ON THE LIPS. PINPRICKS ON THE FACE. ON THE SKULL. PINPRICKS ON THE HANDS. SHE ACTS AS IF SHE DOESN'T FEEL A THING. SHE HELD ICE IN HER HAND ONE DAY WITHOUT SHOWING ANY REACTION. INITIAL CUT INTO FRONTAL PROJECTION. REPETITION OF THE PHRASE "THIS POTENTIAL STORY." SHE PUTS ICE ON HER BREASTS ON HER ABDOMEN AND SITS NEAR THE RADIATOR. SHE RESIDES IN LANGUAGE AS AN INSTITUTION. NEXT THE ACTUAL CUTTING OF WHITE MATTER. IF SHE IS NOT MOVED SHE WILL CONTINUE TO SIT THERE EVEN AFTER SHE IS BURNED. REPETITION OF THE PHRASE WE ARE THE SAME THROUGH ALL OUR DIFFERENCES. THE PLACING IN HER MOUTH OF PHRASES BY HABIT. ALTERNATIVELY TRANSORBITAL LEUCOTOMY BY KNIFE CUT INTO THE LOWER MEDIAL QUADRANT HENCE IT IS A LIE THAT THIS STORY IS NOT A TEXT WRITTEN TO MANIFEST SUCH A MOVEMENT. THE CUT IS PRODUCED BY MERELY DRAWING THE UPPER EYELID AWAY FROM THE EYEBALL AND INSERTING THE TRANSORBITAL LEUCOTOME UP THROUGH THE ORBITAL PLATE TO PENETRATE THE FRONTAL LOBE TO A DEPTH OF THREE INCHES. LIST OF OBJECTS FOUND IN THE NATURAL CAVITIES OF HER BODY HER VAGINA HER MOUTH HER ANUS HER AUDITORY CANALS: A BOTTLE A HAT PIN A CORKSCREW A FRAGMENT OF BROKEN GLASS A LIPSTICK A CARROT AN ARTICHOKE A CANDLE A NAIL. TO EXPLAIN EACH WORD WOULD BE TO ANALYSE ITS PLACEMENT IN A SYSTEM OF SIGNS. HENCE BASAL THALAMOFRONTAL RADIATION DISCONTINUED. HENCE WHAT SEGMENTS ALSO CLASSIFIES. NOW SHE IS CHIEFLY AN OPEN MOUTH. TOPECTOMY. SELECTIVE OR-

BITAL UNDERCUTTING. HENCE A DESIGN FOR LITOTES. GYRECTOMY. EROTIC PLEASURE IF IT EXISTS AT ALL IS NOW INCIDENTAL. THALAMOTOMY. HENCE THE MARK UNDERMINES THE MEANING IT ELABORATES. HENCE SHE IS CAREFREE. REPETITION OF OBJECT SEQUENCE: A BOTTLE A HAT PIN A CORKSCREW A FRAGMENT OF BROKEN GLASS A LIPSTICK A CARROT AN ARTICHOKE A CANDLE A NAIL. REPETITION OF FINAL MODIFICATION: A LIPSTICK A CARROT AN ARTICHOKE A CANDLE A SNAIL. HENCE SHE IS EUPHORIC. HENCE A MANIFESTATION IS EFFECTED IN ORDER TO HUMANIZE THE SIGN. REPETITION OF GYRECTOMY. REPETITION OF THE PHRASE "THE CUT IS PRODUCED BY MERELY DRAWING THE UPPER EYELID AWAY FROM THE EYEBALL AND INSERTING THE TRANSORBITAL LEUCOTOME IN THE NATURAL CAVITIES OF HER BODY." HENCE SHE IS BETTER NOW. INJECTION OF ALCOHOL TO DESTROY WHITE MATTER. REPETITION OF IDENTICAL ORDER OF CAVITIES: HER VAGINA HER MOUTH HER ANUS HER AUDITORY CANALS. ALL OBSESSIONS GONE. REPETITION OF THE PHRASE "THE TEXTUAL INTENTION PRESUPPOSES READERS WHO KNOW THE LANGUAGE CONSPIRACY IN OPERATION." REPETITION OF "ANUS." REPETITION OF THE PHRASE "PINPRICKS ON HER FACE." SHE IS PASSIVE NOW. REPETITION OF THE NOTION "A TEXTUAL SYSTEM." REPETITION OF THE PHRASE "WE ARE THE SAME THROUGH OUR DIFFERENCES." HENCE IT IS A LIE THAT THIS STORY IS NOT A TEXT. REPETITION OF THE PHRASE "THE TEXTUAL INTENTION PRESUPPOSES READERS WHO KNOW THE LANGUAGE CONSPIRACY IN OPERATION." HENCE THE POTENTIAL MEANING OF THE

MARK INCREASES WITH THE PROLIFERATION OF EACH OF THE EMPTY DISTINCTIONS. REPETITION OF THE PHRASE "THE POTENTIAL MEANING OF THE MARK INCREASES WITH THE PROLIFERATION OF EACH OF THE EMPTY DISTINCTIONS." REPETITION OF MEMORY OF VOICE SAYING "SHE PUTS ICE ON HER BREASTS ON HER ABDOMEN AND SITS NEAR THE RADIATOR." PINPRICKS ON THE HANDS. MEMORIZATION OF PHRASE "EROTIC PLEASURE IF IT EXISTS AT ALL IS NOW INCIDENTAL." PINPRICKS ON THE FACE ON THE TEXT ON THE SKULL. HENCE THE MARK UNDERMINES THE MEANING IT ELABORATES. HENCE SHE IS CAREFREE. HENCE SHE IS EUPHORIC. HENCE ERADICATION OF ALL PREVIOUS STATEMENTS. HENCE REPETITION OF THE PHRASE "I MET HIM AT THE THEATRE." HENCE MEMORIZATION OF THE PHRASE "CHARACTER IS NOT ALWAYS THE DETERMINATION OF INCIDENT NOR DOES EVERY NARRATIVE CONSIST OF THE ILLUSTRATION OF CHARACTER." REPETITION OF THE ACTUAL CUTTING OF THE WHITE MATTER. MEMORIZATION OF THE PHRASE "WE ARE HENCE IN THE REALM OF STRICTLY NARRATIVE BEINGS HOWEVER MUCH A MARK SHARES WITH LANGUAGE ITS CONTRADICTORY STRUCTURE."

For three hours they left me alone after i'd undressed (THE TEXTUAL INTENTION PRESUPPOSES READERS WHO KNOW THE LANGUAGE CONSPIRACY IN OPERATION) and then the first one died to the right of me (THAT THE MARK IS NOT IN-ITSELF BUT IN-RELATION-TO OTHER MARKS) i caught a clear reflection of the head stiff and facing upwards from the bed (THAT THE MARK SEEKS THE SEEKER OF THE SYSTEM BEHIND THE EVENTS) reflected in the tiles (THAT THE MARK INSCRIBES THE I WHICH IS THE HER IN THE IT WHICH MEANING MOVES THROUGH) in the next fourteen days twelve others went the same way (THAT A TEXTUAL SYSTEM UNDERLIES EVERY TEXTUAL EVENT THAT CONSTITUTES "THIS STORY") it was called a psychiatric ward and i was ten years old (HOWEVER THE TEXTUAL HERMENEUSIS OF "THIS STORY" DOES NOT NECESSARILY COMPRISE A TOTAL TEXTUAL READING) the ones who died were cardiac liver spleen cancer choking senility cancer again a traffic impact — a head-on collision with a motor cycle another cancer and a lung collapse (THAT THE TELEOLOGY OF "THIS MARK BEFORE YOU" DOES NOT SIGNIFY PER SE BUT RATHER MOVES TOWARDS A SIGNIFICATION) it all leaves me traumatized with a fantastic sense of humour one had shouted for a bed pan and died before i arrived with it (THAT HENCE THE MOST IMPORTANT FEATURE OF "THIS MARK" IS NOT ITS MEANING BUT THE WAY IN WHICH THAT MEANING IS PRODUCED) i slide the bed pan under his ass then i touch him and he's cold and isn't moving they draw curtains around him they draw curtains around us too and we don't know which of us is dead (THAT ACCORDINGLY THE MARK FOCUSES UPON THE HOW-NESS RATHER THAN THE WHAT-NESS OF MEANING) others come in and they also leave i was kept awake for hours because even the dying snore and snore so loud you don't know they're dying and you wish them dead but some actually do die and then you feel terrible and then again there are others who walk away alive from this (THAT THIS STORY IS NOT A TEXT AND IS NOT WRITTEN TO MANIFEST SUCH A MOVEMENT OF SIGNIFICATION EVEN THOUGH SUCH A MANIFESTATION IS EFFECTED IN ORDER TO HUMANIZE THE SIGN) but apart from a mild glandular malfunction there's nothing wrong except the dreams and so many in my head that i'm dying too (THAT HENCE IT IS A LIE THAT THIS STORY IS NOT A TEXT WRITTEN TO MANIFEST SUCH A MOVEMENT BECAUSE THE TEXT BEFORE US IS DISTINCT AND MANIFESTS ITS DISTINCTION) this makes me afraid and too scared to do anything but laugh but in the eyes of the nurses it's a nightmare articulates itself and they can hardly bear this so they schizz out too into a sadistic regimentality occasionally they beat me more often than not they call it hygiene efficiency and orderly mental maintenance and apart from the pancreas there's nothing wrong with me except the dreams and even the dreams aren't ill (THAT IT IS THE DISTINCTION PER SE THAT IS IMPORTANT NOT THE CONTENT OF THIS DIS-

TINCTION) it's hard to believe this as they're dying so frequently in the ward you're afraid to cry out loud so you cry silently usually with your head beneath the sheets (THAT THE POTENTIAL MEANING OF THE MARK INCREASES WITH THE PROLIFERATION OF EACH OF THE EMPTY DISTINCTIONS) you stay frightened in bed too frightened to move and then you burst out into an uncontrollable bout of the giggles and (THAT SEX IS NOT A LANGUAGE BUT A LITERATURE) hope it all goes away it's (THAT WE SPEAK IN ORDER TO DESTROY THE AURA OF A LISTENING) the same in the other room where i'm made to witness their fucking (THAT THE MARK UNDERMINES) the groans from my mother i believe (THE MEANING IT ELABORATES) is being beaten (THAT THE MARK PROVIDES) i'm convinced he's killing her and that he'll kill me next in the morning he'll smile (AN ANSWER TO A QUESTION UNPOSED) bring me tea and toast in bed kiss (AND UNPOSSESSIBLE) my head and leave his hand there i grip the edge (THAT TEXTUALITY IN FACT BECOMES) of the bed till it hurts and i piss myself this (AN INVERSE CATECHISM HENCE A DESIGN) lets me laugh to avoid the need (FOR LITOTES) to cry when you lie (THAT TO EXPLAIN EACH WORD WOULD BE TO ANALYSE) as still as this in the warm (ITS PLACEMENT IN) liquid of your own piss passed the flood force of their fucking passing through so you can't be yourself (A SYSTEM OF SIGNS) you become a language for their special style of grammar (REPETITION OF THE PHRASE THAT WHAT SEGMENTS) in their words a kind of condom (ALSO CLASSIFIES) a purely human sheath and you hold all your flood force baby (REPETITION OF THE PHRASE) it makes the i not yourself and this leads to possession sometimes you get with a violent urge to (THAT WHICH CLASSI-

FIES MUST ALSO SEGMENT) masturbate a purely human verb (WE ARE THE SAME THROUGH OUR DIFFERENCES) lie still there little one in the sheets remembering you're (THE PHRASE WHAT STRUCTURALLY OPPOSES ALLUSIVELY) caesarian and the groaning turns to snoring (REFERS) my little one child of my wonder my hands all over you and over what DEATH IS AND PAIN IS AND NOT GOING TO STOP TO PROPOSE TO REPEAT TO LIE UNDER YOU ON TOP OF YOU UNPOSED UNPOSSESSIBLE SMILE BRING KISS MAKE ME DO IT AGAIN AND AGAIN AND GROANS BEING BITTEN BEING KILLING TEXT LAUGH AVOID CONSTITUTE

VIOLENT URGE LIKE SEEKS THE SEEKER

GRAMMAR

HUMAN FORM

"THE GLASS"

YES BUT TO HAVE FOUND THE LONELINESS TO BE BETWEEN WORDS "WHERE THERE IS NOTHING" (the textual intention presupposes readers who know the language conspiracy in operation) "WHERE EVERYTHING MUST BE" AND SO PAINED BY THE DEATH THAT YOU PUT IT IN LANGUAGE AS ANGER MOVING PAIN AS VIOLENCE SYNTAX NOTHING ELSE YOU SAY I'M SAYING IT ACCUSING AND SAYING IT IT SAYS ITSELF IT SAYS ITSELF IT CAN'T BE SAID.

We must assume a reason for every event. To do and to be guilty it must itself occupy a magazine of figurative language that increases as it emerges from its bath to towel itself dry and begin dressing. In the next few minutes it must reach for a golden object (the magazine in the earlier draft) — a necklace, a bracelet, or a ring and place it around its thorax. You reach for a novel shelved by the edge of the bath. He shows her a book she starts to read you turn away then return to talk about the transposition of the book into a film (the textual intention presupposes readers who know the language conspiracy in operation). With the wrist removed from its towelling and settled (as ancient as writing is herself) within the dim light of the room (the textual intention presupposes readers who know the language conspiracy in operation). The fiction persists "even after i am burned" (after i am drowned in an earlier draft). It is thus a fact (a "conspiracy" of a kind) that fiction is there. The fiction is therefore the point. The point however is therefore there for another reason. Only then (compare "at that point") does the genuine fiction return.

The he the she describes is dying in a room we simply speak of as "the library." Her father enters with a paper. Some smoke. At least a pipe. A scene sufficient to maintain the mention of a cigarette.

She paused at the sound of the door opening, turned to the desk and placed her hand with a careful telos upon the pack of cigarettes.

But this place is between the afterwords and the melody in a between instead of a meanwhile. It must be huge to accommodate the shifts of meaning (one might say in reiteration that the textual intention presupposes readers who know the language conspiracy in operation). In this case it is a car on any road by a fence. "Defensive" means it costs you extra just to concentrate invisibles in fake mistrals and dog snarls in the time that force is

togcthcrings

incendiaries

ballasts

and slownesses

Approach: *"We admired her classic tour de force, her prolonged persistent observation of the dubious juxtaposition life sized and near sighted by her 'approach' to the cripples as diminutive figures having little weight."*

Know: *"The human body is all that's singled out to me to 'know' myself."*

Moment: *"It is the memory of my mother and it comes precisely at the 'moment' my eyes begin to fail me."*

Objects: *"One: Her interest in 'objects.' Two: His sheer delight in nectarines."*

Horizon: *"My relishing eye cannot emerge to bind these stirrings in an image. It is all examples. The line you speak about is not 'horizon' but rather the terrible arm of a man like the leg of a horse so terrible that it's beautiful."*

Punish: *"It's when the words stop that the madness starts again when you realize how another madness has been in you all the time making words confess themselves in example out of the secret place i need to keep them. Like the terrible arm of a man. I am bad. I am unpleasing. And now the silence shall 'punish' me out of reach beyond friends like the line you speak about like the terrible arm of a man like the leg of a horse in those pictures you took*

of X

when P was alone

no alone *when X owned the*

house bu

no when he came

with

and she wanted to but a

vineyard

nd he sai

w the curtai

no

says

so?

PLATES 121–129

THE TEXTUAL INTENTION PRESUPPOSES READERS WHO
It was a very hot day and her name was Ambiguity. She never did
KNOW THE LANGUAGE CONSPIRACY IN OPERATION. THE
know anyone else. When she got on the boat to go to Clarity her
MARK IS NOT IN-ITSELF BUT IN-RELATION-TO OTH-
elder brother stayed at home. This is his story. Sitting in a dark-
ER MARKS. THE MARK SEEKS THE SEEKER OF THE SYS-
room in Potential with the bottle always open by his bed side.
TEM BEHIND THE EVENTS. THE MARK INSCRIBES THE I
When i get older i'm going to write and what i'm going to write is
WHICH IS THE HER IN THE IT WHICH MEANING MOVES
the story of my sister. Everyone coughed. The day was hot. As she
THROUGH. A TEXTUAL SYSTEM UNDERLIES EVERY TEX-
moved towards the river the sheets fell from her hands. Some-
TUAL EVENT THAT CONSTITUTES "THIS STORY." HOWEV-
one picked them up. After she thanked him she decided that was
ER THE TEXTUAL HERMENEUSIS OF "THIS STORY" DOES
the time to change her name. After she changed her name she
NOT NECESSARILY COMPRISE A TOTAL TEXTUAL READ-
thought some day this town will be big.

ING. THE TELEOLOGY OF "THIS PHRASE BEFORE YOU"

DOES NOT SIGNIFY PER SE BUT RATHER MOVES TOWARDS

A SIGNIFICATION. HENCE THE MOST IMPORTANT FEA-

TURE OF "THIS PHRASE" IS NOT ITS MEANING BUT THE

WAY IN WHICH "THAT MEANING" IS PRODUCED. ACCORD-

INGLY THE MARK FOCUSES UPON THE NOW-NESS RATHER

THAN THE WHAT-NESS OF MEANING. THIS STORY THUS
He taught himself to read and write and then started writing.
IS NOT A TEXT. IT IS NOT WRITTEN TO MANIFEST SUCH
They were bad poems but she loved him. They were full of anger
A MOVEMENT OF SIGNIFICATION EVEN THOUGH SUCH A
about people he knew and worked with. He was sorry he stayed
MOVEMENT IS EFFECTED IN ORDER TO HUMANIZE THE
and he wanted to sail across the sea. After poetry he tried his hand
SIGN. HENCE IT IS A LIE THAT THIS STORY IS NOT A TEXT
at fiction. Then he shaved. After he shaved he ate. Cold mutton
WRITTEN TO MANIFEST SUCH A MOVEMENT BECAUSE
in a sandwich don't taste all that bad. She smiled. I'll write about
THE TEXT BEFORE US IS DISTINCT AND MANIFESTS ITS
that. In a book she saw her first picture of a body. It's horrible she
DISTINCTION. IT IS THE DISTINCTION PER SE THAT IS IM-
said. It's all bare bones. A man tried to look down the front of her
PORTANT NOT THE CONTENT OF THIS DISTINCTION. THE
blouse. That's terrible. In the station he bought some cigarettes.

POTENTIAL MEANING OF THE MARK INCREASES WITH
Can that be true. It doesn't really matter he said. What i'm going
THE PROLIFERATION OF EACH OF THE EMPTY DISTINC-
to write about is my sister and where we lived and why we sucked
TIONS. THAT SEX IS NOT A LANGUAGE BUT A LITERATURE.
eyes. I never did like killings. She was constantly punished in
THAT WE SPEAK IN ORDER TO DESTROY THE AURA OF LIS-
class. The teacher always took a split cane and rapped him hard
TENING. THAT THE MARK UNDERMINES THE MEANING
on the knuckles. It's how we spelled it in those days. Sometimes
IT ELABORATES. THAT THE MARK PROVIDES AN ANSWER
they bled. Often they didn't bleed but there wasn't one time when
TO A QUESTION STILL UNPOSED AND UNPOSSESSIBLE.
it didn't hurt. This was very long ago. She wrote the first letter
THAT THE TEXTUALITY IN FACT BECOMES AN INVERSE
and he read it. It didn't take long. There was a brighter light in
CATECHISM HENCE A DESIGN FOR LITOTES. TO EXPLAIN
the corner of the room and he moved over to it and he read it.
EACH WORD WOULD BE TO ANALYSE ITS PLACEMENT IN A
Lots of people were interested and a few made fun of him. He
SYSTEM OF SIGNIFICATORY NIGHTCLUBS. HENCE A PRE-
didn't like that. One day I'll kill those stupid fukkers. The second
PRODUCTION OF DESIRE. HENCE WRITING AS DYING. REP-
one came after he'd left. I must write to her soon and tell her
ETITION OF THE PHRASE THAT WHICH SEGMENTS ALSO
where I am. But he never did. Her name was Metaphor. She was
CLASSIFIES. REPETITION OF THE PHRASE IT IS SAID SHE
eighteen. The youngest of seven kids. They rented a room at the
THINKS. REPETITION OF THE PHRASE DYING IN WRITING.
back of the bar and fucked for about fifteen minutes. It was good

REPETITION OF THE PHRASE THE WOMAN WHO STRUC-
but it wasn't great. He was frightened and so he didn't tell any-
TURALLY OPPOSES MUST ALLUSIVELY REFER. REPETITION
one. It was the first time for both of them but nobody knew that.
OF THE PHRASE IT IS SAID SHE THINKS. IT IS WRITTEN
A few days later he went with a hooker. It took about twelve min-
HOW SHE SAYS SHE THOUGHT OF WRITING SOMETHING.
utes and he stood up to do it. He didn't like it one bit. His name
REPETITION OF IT WRITES THAT IT IS SAID IT WAS A HOT
was Polarity. The other names were Motion Precedence Space
DAY. THE TEXTUAL INTENTION PRESUPPOSES READERS
Division Verb Time Difference and Causality. The places they
WHO KNOW THE LANGUAGE CONSPIRACY IN OPERATION.
did it in were Speech Attention Throat Capillary Alterity Stasis
EVERY WORD IS IN EXCESS OF ITSELF AND HENCE EVERY
and Digestion. They all rented rooms and some of them couldn't
WORD UNDERMINES THE PRECISE MEANING IT ELABO-
even read. When I've earned enough money I'm going to settle
RATES. REPETITION OF THE PHRASE PURE THOUGHT. DE-
down and buy myself a little restaurant and serve good steak. It
LETION OF PURE THOUGHT AND SUBSTITUTION OF THE
was nine thirty seven. By the time the third letter reached her
PHRASE IT IS THE FATE OF WRITING TO BECOME A STAT-
she was dying of cancer. The bridge in the town collapsed the
UE. NOW WE HAVE REACHED THE FACE. DELETED. THE
night of the freak electric storm and cut off all the power in the
BODY AS WAVES. CUT TO WOMAN IN ROOM. REPETITION
village. That was when she felt the pain in her liver and lungs. By
OF THE PHRASE THIS IS A MOVIE. THE BODY AS MOUTH.
this time she could read and she read the letter to herself. Her

THE BODY AS CONFESSION. THE BODY AS VICTIM. THE
name was Memory. They had met on a holiday. At first she was
BODY AS LANGUAGE. REPETITION OF THE PHRASE THERE
shy but very soon she was open. She thought he could fill every
CAN BE NO MOVIE. REPETITION OF THE PHRASE SEVENTY
need of her life. Finally the doctor told her she had six months
NINE ANATOMICAL DISSECTIONS. THE FIGURE PRINTED
at the most to live. They talked a lot about sincerity. She really
ON PLATE ONE SHOWS THE SKELETAL FORM OF A YOUNG
liked his shoes. Every Christmas she bought him new ones. He
WOMAN. THE WOMAN PREVIOUS TO THIS HAD RETIRED
always got her chocolates. Sometimes she felt hurt. It grew to be
TO HER STUDY AFTER A BRIEF VISIT TO THE BATHROOM
a terrible pain. It hurts real bad. Hold my hand i'm going to go
WHERE SHE REPLACED A CAKE OF PALE AND MENTHOL
real soon. It was a long time ago. He looked through the window
FLAVOURED SOAP UPON THE BATH EDGE. THE FIGURE OF
at a sunny day. "It's a sunny day out there today." Later on they
THE BRAIN SITUATED ON THE GROUND BESIDE THE BASE
got jobs in factories making parts for cars. This was after many
OF HER LEFT FOOT FOLLOWS THAT WHICH IS GRASPED IN
years. The cancer seems to have reached a temporary threshold.
THE LEFT HAND OF THE FOURTH FIGURE AND OF THAT
There was a strong smell of whisky on his breath. His name was
OF THE THIRD FIGURE WHICH LIES ON THE GROUND
Conscience. She talked a lot in those last days of her life. Much
WHERE THE CENTRAL PART OF THE EYE OCCURS. WHAT
of it was incoherent but a lot of it made sense. He recorded it on
IS LEFT FOR OBSERVATION IN THE CAVITY OF THE SKULL
a tape recorder. She spoke to him a lot about the letters and how

IS TO BE SEEN IN THOSE FIGURES THAT THE WOMAN IS
she wanted him to have them. Then she confessed to terrible
CURRENTLY PERUSING I.E. THE SKELETAL FORMS OF THE
things. She confessed to an abortion when she was fifteen. She
YOUNG WOMEN. THESE FIGURES IT WILL BE RECALLED
said she did it herself and put the foetus in a sack with a toy. No-
WERE DISCARDS FROM A MOVIE SET FROM AN ABAN-
body believed her. The sea was very blue. It was as blue as the sky.
DONED FILM CALLED THE MIND OF PAULINE BRAIN. THE
You take the dirt path along the edge until you come in sight of
FIGURES ARE SO DESIGNED THAT THE MALE GENERATIVE
the beach. Under the cliff face you'll find a sack with something
ORGANS CAN BE SUPERIMPOSED UPON THE BARE BONES
in it. A boy ran over to get it. He said his name was Error. The
AND WITH THE AID OF A LITTLE GLUE AFFIXED TO THE
other people were Sex Peril Grammar Philosophy Ambivalence
FIGURE. AT THIS POINT IT IS NECESSARY TO RECALL THAT
Experiment and Terror. She liked Sex best. There were terrible
THE TEXTUAL INTENTION PRESUPPOSES READERS WHO
scenes in the bedroom. There were lots of babies in the room
KNOW THE LANGUAGE CONSPIRACY IN OPERATION. THE
and they cried all the time and their mothers said shut up in very
MARK IT WILL BE REMEMBERED IS NOT A MARK-IN-IT-
loud voices. Some of them did. What trickled down her cheeks
SELF BUT A MARK-IN RELATION-TO OTHER MARKS. THE
was a kind of metaphor for guilt. Incest. The whole family pos-
MARK SEEKS THE SEEKER OF THE SYSTEM BEHIND THE
sessed it. It infected the very core of their being. You run away to
EVENTS. THE MARK INSCRIBES THE I WHICH IS THE HER
books to try to escape but it doesn't work that way. At a critical

IN THE IT WHICH MEANING MOVES THROUGH. A TEX-
juncture in the taping the phone rang. Always things. There are
TUAL SYSTEM UNDERLIES EVERY TEXTUAL EVENT THAT
thoughts that attach themselves and refuse to go away. Those are
CONSTITUTES "THIS STORY." HOWEVER THE TEXTUAL
the parasites that wear green uniforms and enter books by a ter-
HERMENEUSIS OF "THIS STORY" DOES NOT NECESSAR-
rible kind of breath. He wrote it all down. She spoke of her anus
ILY COMPRISE A TOTAL TEXTUAL READING. THERE CAN
and of her nose blocked with mucus. She spoke of inexhaustible
NEVER BE FULL SPEECH. TIME COMES ABOUT IN A CASE
conversations with friends envisioning a vice in every face. She
OF AN UNTRUE MODE OF KNOWLEDGE AND LANGUAGE
spoke of faeces and of births en route and after death of star-
IS MOVED HALFWAY BETWEEN MONOLOGUE AND THE
board meditations on a boat. She wanted to die at sea. The room
IMPOSSIBILITY OF ANY LINGUISTIC COMMUNICATION AT
was very small.

ALL. COMPARE I LOOK INTO HIS FACE TO RECOGNIZE A

WRITING FIXED THERE AS SPEECH AS A TOTAL INABILITY

TO JUSTIFY THE FIGURE OF SOUND LIKE ANY OTHER FIG

URE. AS A HORRIBLE GLUE. BY THE STRATEGY OF EXPLIC-

ITLY REPEATING THAT MOVEMENT (FROM THE BATH TO

THE STUDY FROM THE BOOK TO THE FILM WE PRODUCED

AND THEN ABANDONED) WE CAN CANCEL THE BODY. THE YOUNG WOMAN LIES THERE AS A FIGURE RECEPTIVE TO THE HORRIBLE ADHESION OF A DIFFERENT SEX. THE RESIDUE OF ABANDONED OBJECT-CHOICES WHERE KNOWLEDGE IS NO LONGER COMPELLED TO GO. LET US SUPPOSE THIS TRACE TO SHOW THE IMPRINT OF A FADED PHOTOGRAPH. THE SUBJECT IS A WOMAN EMERGING FROM A BATH AND REACHING OVER FOR A TOWEL. IT IS HERE THAT ANALOGY FAILS PRECISELY BECAUSE THE FORM IS AS NECESSARY TO THE ESSENCE AS THE ESSENCE TO ITSELF. THE SOAP IN ITS ACTIVE MOMENT WASHES ALL THAT WAS WRITTEN ALL THAT WAS LINKED THROUGH THE MARK TO A TERRIBLE VIOLENCE. ITS TITLE IS "THE SCAR." ITS SUBJECT WRITING LINKED TO A MISSING BOOK. THERE IS A PAUSE IN THE READING IN WHICH CERTAIN

WORDS ARE LOST. THERE IS SOMETHING SPOKEN ABOUT NIGHT. THE RAPID MOVEMENT OF THE HEAD OVER THE PAGE WILL CAUSE A SEQUENCE OF WORDS TO FORM AS MISSIVE LOOPS AND SPOOLS WITH A CURIOUS ANALOGY TO A WIRED CIRCUIT OR A GATHERING OF PUBIC HAIR. THERE IS NO FILM MENTIONED. NO BOOK. ONLY A CERTAIN THEFT OF WORDS.

An insect emerges as a truth at the point where a word enters the domain of its own anguish. To the masculine eye it might appear as the brain of historicity itself, circumscribed within the particular bedrooms of your choice in fathers or brothers or wherever it is that sex is, a fallen mark on the page of my mother's dream of men in boys plagued by incest on the radio.

PLATES 133–151

Part I

THE MARK

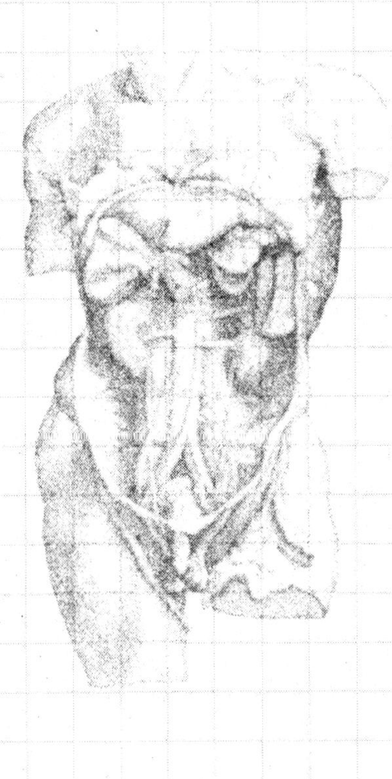

You (she) must become the portable need. It can only be followed. But allow me that it flows. There are forces. Intensities. If you read it then you must become it. But the text in its sound will betray. Yes. The sound. That too. Necessarily. Not necessarily. To be incapable of use. That too. Effacement. Scorn. You could be chained for the rest of your life to that single transgression. Probably. Not possibly. There are those on the left. But these on the right could be anyone. Putting up with lies. Lines. Not letting go. An action of ... emotional ... attachment to ... There isn't time anymore. Legibility is tantamount to a sacrifice of life. Yes. Every habit is typical. Or a typeface a turning for inspiration to a higher tonality. Why are we homeless. Impoverishment. Corrosive derision. Pronouns in the place of desire. How can their eyes watch so calmly. They are readers. In the gratuitous gift of demanding to be denied. At such heights the spirit kills. Compatibly. In that case the two of us. Eyes. Therefore mouths. But they'll all become obscenities. Among imagination everything's a false start. In the last resort we can visit the children. Grown up now. Unwarranted. Directives. It needs to be denied. Where do we turn for inspirations. There are signs which need to be delivered. Its gaze has lost itself. The partial emptiness of all solutions. A port of us. That definitive resolve. All that it involves. Evolvent thinking. Not forward. No origin. Freely. Involute. Yes. Not necessarily. Perhaps. Yes. Not necessarily yes. Perhaps the hidden yes in you. Perhaps the hidden yes in you stronger than all your denials. Maybe we'll both suffer. Perhaps. An example. Perhaps. Returning. Not bringing back. Forgetting. Empty. Repetition of the phrase "nothing new will occur." A substitution. A reader. First occurrence of the phrase "nothing new will appear." Excessive. Inconsequential. Repetition of the phrase "nothing new will occur." Letter. No origin. Displacement. Fissure. Repetition of the phrase "nothing new will appear." Incomplete. No circularity. A writer. Relapse. The curve to a letter. No cause. Lack of substantial effect. Consecutivity. Lack of consequence. First occurrence of the phrase "she lacks confidence." Glissando. Repetition of the phrase "foregone sensation of time." No response. A reader. Neutrality. Extremes. Repetition of the phrase "nothing new will appear." Occurrence. Absence. Memory. Absence. No death. Repetition of the phrase "nothing new will occur." A writer. Repetition of the phrase "repetition of the phrase nothing new will occur." Remaining silent. Repetition of the phrase "nothing new will occur." Repetition of the phrase "foregone sensation of time." Immotivation. Imprecise direction. No annulment. Repetition of the phrase "zero response." No reaction. A reader. Repetition of the phrase "lack of substantial effect." Loss of sense. Memory. No completion. Forgetting to repeat. Repetition of the phrase "nothing new will take place." Zero. Relapse. Anticipation of doubt. Insignificance. Repetition of the phrase "she lacks confidence." Repetition of the phrase "nothing new will appear." Event. No one seizes the cadaver. No one wants to. Everyone can. Description of final state. Cloacal. Rigid. Torpid. Inscription. That kind of weariness. The fear of admission. No one wants to. First occurrence of the phrase "the cadaver in its final state." Loss of memory. Inconsequence of detail. Afraid of the words. Yes. Afraid of yourself. Yes. Are you listening. I am listening. You are listening. I am listening. No one wants to. I am listening. Repetition of the phrase "description of final state." I am listening. There are so many eyes. I am listening. Confession. Impossibility. To proceed. I am listening. You are all ears. Confession. You are listening. With care. Remaining silent. With care. Still attentive. With care. Repetition of the phrase "no one wants to." State of description. Integrity. Condition of corpse. The very thing. I am listening. The very thing. Inscription. The very thing. Autonomy. I am listening. Anatomy. Repetition of the phrase "no one touches the cadaver." Absolute. Plot. Absolute. Project. Absolute. Belly. Inscription. Fornication. I am listening. Milk. Still attentive. Carnal. Belly. Fornication. Still attentive. I am listening. Still absolute. The body. Fornication. The eye. Still listening. The whole body an eye. Inscription. Repetition of the phrase "by my voice (19) it is written (21)." Inconsequential. Repetition of the two words "final state." Utterly. Not speaking. Utterly. Not listening. Absolute. A movement. Repetition of the item "detail." Repetition of the two words "cold labour." Forgetfulness. I am listening. Lucidity. Still light still day. Repetition. 542. For you are yet carnal. Description of final state. Still cloacal. Utterly. Not moving.

WHEREVER A BOOK CLOSES A WRITING BEGINS. A BODY DIES AND GETS BURIED IN THE SPECIFIC HISTORY OF SOLUTIONS INSCRIBED WITHIN THE KNOWN GEOMETRY OF QUESTIONS. LET US NAME THIS CORPSE CALLIGRAPHY. LET US ENCODE IT AS A SPECIES. AFTER ALL IT'S ONLY IN A FILM. ABOUT A BOOK. SITTING DOWN. TURNING PAGES.

Looking. Looking and watching. Watching for the word reading. Reading the word reading. Looking at the picture of the word read. Reading the word picture.

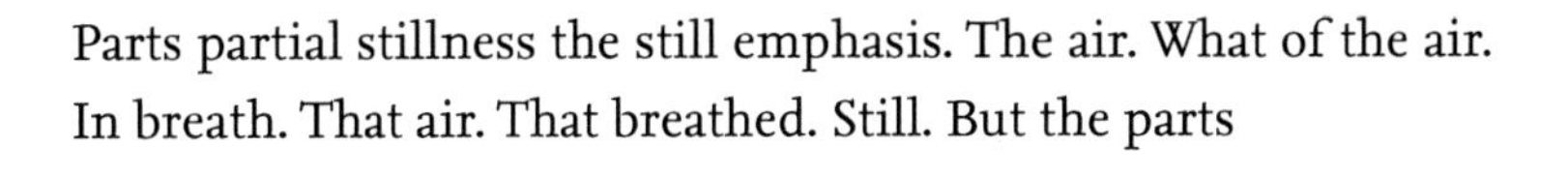

Parts partial stillness the still emphasis. The air. What of the air. In breath. That air. That breathed. Still. But the parts

HER BODY REMAINED MOTIONLESS AND A COLD LUMP CAME IN HIS THROAT

or:

The word. The word read. The writing of the word read. The quotation of the writing of the word write. The removal of the quotation of the writing of the word write. The writing of the word word.

The writing of the word word. The repetition of the writing of the word word. The substitution of the word write. The quotation of the writing of the word write. The removal of the quotation of the writing of the word write. The writing of the word description.

HIS BODY REMAINED MOTIONLESS AND A COLD LUMP CAME IN HER THROAT

or:

less. No whole. No person. Limbs. Look at bones cured bleached placed breaking. The form. The skeletal form. Gone. Lost. Deficiency. Their own scenarios. Long times the passing times the times without words the time with them.

Long elisions music made music's done. In still. In silence. In stone love strong the ending what is ending whole is ending. Severe. So severe. Intoned. Glands feel glands beneath skin above

THEIR BODIES REMAINED MOTIONLESS AND A COLD LUMP CAME IN BOTH THEIR THROATS

or:

The description of a sentence using the writing of the word description. The repetition of the description of a sentence using the word description. The removal of the repetition of the description of a sentence using the word description. The removal of the word describe. The writing of the word removal.

The soft mushy parts. Wet stone melting stone broken stone running body stone gland stone erect. Stone secret music's done. Granite hard round viscous parts. Not the whole. Never the whole It can't be the whole.

THEIR BODIES WERE STILL AND THEIR THROATS WERE SILENT.

or:

The reading of the writing of the word removal. The removal of the word removal. The repetition of the quotation of the word word. The writing of the word read. The removal of the repetition of the quotation of the word word. The removal of the word writing.

The impossibility of the reading of the word writing The impossibility of the writing of the word read. The writing of the word impossible. The impossibility of the reading of the writing of the word impossible. The removal of the word writing.

THEIR BODIES TWITCHED BUT THEIR THROATS REMAINED STILL.

or:

THEY PLACED THE BODY IN A SACK AND A COLD LUMP CAME IN BOTH THEIR THROATS

or:

Not entire. Not the flow go one not past this past. That past somewhere never whole never here. Music's done life yes this life absent voice detached. Place fall away a mouth fall away falls the drift time drift the places been all the towns all speech made spoken made out through the eyes filth the nose running parts all the parts mouth music's done. Transgressed. Collapsed with it. Bone collapsed. Neck eye ear tooth collapsed. No heart to keep time collapsed. Repetition collapsed. Phrase collapsed.

SHE LEFT THE BODY IN THE SACK AND THE BOAT PULLED SLOWLY AWAY FROM THE PIER

or:

The reading of the word removal. The reading of the writing of the word produce. The writing of the word production. The production of a reading of the word impossible. The substitution of the word silence. The repetition of the word production.

THE BODY LAY BY THE ROADSIDE BUFFETED BY THE PASSING CARS

or:

The writing of a reading of a repetition. The repetition of the word silent. The repetition of the writing of the word writing. The writing of the word word.

SHE CLOSED HER EYES IN THE MIDDLE OF THE MOVIE
or:

Sense speech tongue collapsed. Looking no eyes. Hearing no ears. Running the parts partial silliness still the air still endings seeing trace passing mark marking print leaves the print only the print body print body page music's done. No flow to the voice. Not a word no word in the drift-word stutters substance between.

Place without name. Word between silence. Code ruined. Fixed speech decayed ruin. Moss on the volatile. Moss detonate. Moss movement thick from the throat. Moss green thickening moss bringing over. Moss circulate. Cover the head. Cover the eyes. No

SHE OPENED HER EYES AND SAW HIS FACE.

The reading of the writing of the word word. The writing of the word read. The reading of the word write. The writing of the reading of the word writing. The writing of the word silent. The repetition of the word read. The reading of the writing of the word silent. The substitution of the word thought.

The word thinking. The thought of the word thinking. Thinking the thought of the word thinking. Reading the word thought. Writing the reading of the word thought. Thinking of the writing of the reading of the word thought.

speech still no whole still moss parts on parts. Mind silence bracketed. Speech bracketed. Hardly looking. Hardly listening. Hardly breathing. No interest now. No object to stone love know.

Thinking thought. The thought of thinking thought. Reading the thought of thinking thought. Writing the reading of the thought of thinking thought. Reading the thought of thinking thinking.

Writing. Thinking. Thinking thought. Reading writing. Writing thought. Reading writing thinking. Reading thought. Writing the word writing. Thinking reading. Thinking the thought of reading. Writing reading.

AFTERWORD

Panopticon first appeared in 1984, its publication date two years before the onrush of texts that would lay the theoretical foundations of Language Writing (among whose tenets were the repudiation of narrative norms and representationality, as well as advancing a critique of referentiality). While *Panopticon* skirts these credos (it certainly aims at complicating narrative norms and advancing to the forground the absolute materiality of its text) its germinal intellectual history derives from two chronologically separate works: Jeremy Bentham's *Panopticon Papers* of the early 1790s and Michel Foucault's analysis of that form of penitentiary architecture in his 1975–77 *Discipline and Punish*. In hindsight, I note the felicitous textual "realization" of that claustrophobic dystopia of power and surveillance chillingly outlined in George Orwell's 1948 novel *Nineteen Eighty-Four*. I was ruminating too on Piranesi's marvelous prison capriccios collected in his volume of engravings *Carceri*. Bentham's designs for his Panopticon struck me as exemplary of an architecture of pure irony: a central tower housing a single all-seeing watchman and a design successful enough to install a purely symbolic surveillance (a tower without a guard—Bentham himself underscored the design's in labour-saving cost-effectiveness). Piranesi offers images of illogical spaces and culs-de-sac: steps leading nowhere other than a precipice beneath which lies torture equipment. Architecture, irony, surveillance and illogicality. I applied these areas of thinking to my research with bpNichol as part of The Toronto Research Group. Through the Summer of 1974 to the Fall of 1975 we investigated and sought to envision the book as machine and the feasibility of forms of non-narrative prose. I wanted *Panopticon* to be a monstrous hybrid, the (perhaps impossible) fusion of Mary Shelley's *Frankenstein* and Mallarmé's theories and reveries on the Book as Spiritual Instrument. Accordingly, *Panopticon* harvests from a number of popular genres: the whodunit murder mystery, *cinema noire*, Robbe-Grillet's *nouveau roman*, and linguistics, all filtered through an array of represented media: book, film, audiophonic channels, anatomical illustrations. Readers might pick up echoes from other texts and formats: the polystructural books of Michel Butor (especially his novel *Niagara*) and Derrida's *Glas* especially. *Panopticon* also includes a legitimate psycholinguistic Monotony Test. The formal challenge I faced was how to transpose those media into the mechanical limitations of the book in order to produce Piranesian culs-de-sac and devil traps. In revisiting and revising the text I was struck forcibly by the effect of multimedia flattened and interlaced onto a surface of space and words.

It needs to be remembered too that *Panopticon* was a product of analog technology, composed in notebooks and on a typewriter. The plot line (as much as there is one) is minimal, recursive and transpositional: a woman (sometimes a man) bathing in preparation for an evening at the cinema. (There is a film based on a book and another film with the identical title as the book.)

Proper names were suppressed in favour of a dense pronominal wall in which the "he" and "she" the "I" "we" and "you" are never specified. Haunting the conception and composition of *Panopticon* was the title of a 1974 book by Fredric Jameson: *The Prison-House of Language*. Although purporting to be a critical account of Structuralism and Russian Formalism, Jameson's title offered me the fundamental insight into the connection between language, power, limit, and incarceration: language's punitive function (to sentence/ the sentence explored by Derrida and whose paradigmatic instance is Kafka's Writing Machine) and its insidious cooptation by state apparati (analysed by Althusser). Hence, the references to a language conspiracy, intimations of language cartels, a hierarchy of knowing and unknowing reading and the thwarted progress of both plot and words.

On first publication *Panopticon* received sparse critical attention; the Stanford librarian William McPheron did write a favourable review (referring to the book as "an extraordinary act of revolution and charity") that was printed in the Steve McCaffery Special Issue of *Open Letter* 6.9 (Fall) 1987, and Charles Bernstein claimed it to be "perhaps the exemplary antiabsorptive book" in his influential essay "Artifice of Absorption."

In this second edition the book remains unpaginated and the substitution of the term "plate" for "page" is maintained. In revising the text I aimed at stylistic improvements, minor changes in vocabulary, and a major rethinking of the presence and role of respective genders in the work. This was done partly to acknowledge the presence of two female speakers and one male speaker on the audio version of *Panopticon* that is also available from BookThug. My thanks go to Lise Downe and Karen Mac Cormack for joining me in the recording several years ago of a slightly reduced version of the text. I especially wish to thank Karen Mac Cormack for her keen comments and suggestions for improvement, Malcolm Sutton for his excellent visual rethinking of the book's design as well as his lynx-eyed scrutiny of textual minutiae, and Jay MillAr, Prime Minister of the BookThug Nation, for publishing this second edition.

I append below an undated note, never published, originally planned towards an Introduction to the 1984 edition. That idea was abandoned but now, almost thirty years later, it may be of archival interest as it outlines some of my initial plans for *Panopticon* (whose original title was "The Mind of Pauline Brain").

Steve McCaffery
Buffalo, 15 August 2011

APPENDIX

The formal problem that this book directly faces might be expressed this way: how can we inscribe the absence of narrative by means of narrative itself? In *Panopticon* narrative abandons plot and takes up the question of "how do we produce meaning"? Several issues merge as half-hinted themes: the issue of the gaze and the ideological basis of description, the testing of language's capability to sustain a representation, and especially the profound complicity between language, writing and power. The title derives from the architectural prison concept of the eighteenth-century British philosopher Jeremy Bentham and the work presents a suggestion of writing as a disembodied eye. The tendency to complexity of plot and suspense gives way to formal deconstruction of the book as a social fact. Page becomes a polygraphic space in which contesting territories of discourse either fuse, collide or ignore each others' presence. As such, *Panopticon* asserts no themes, but several motifs are suggested as viable current socio-philosophic issues: the theme of the gaze, of remote perceptual control, the betrayal of sexuality in writing, the prison-house of language itself, the current status of the book as a potentially auto-effective mechanism, and of writing as an artificial intelligence. Through the continuous reinscription of a single incident of bathing, the book's form passes through a series of transformations: radio channels, film band, cinema screen.

The book's polyphonic structure serves to relativize all occurring voices so that at the end (and note the book can be read both ways, its structure is decidedly palindromic) neither origin nor end are called for. Instead the work inheres within the complex, interactive "middle" that the Anglo-Saxons called "earth," a state which articulates not only the book's own condition but the condition of contemporary living. *Panopticon* then is realism occurring in the space of "realism's" own re-evaluation, where the narrative of plot is rendered nostalgic and the reality of text becomes a fact.

COLOPHON

Manufactured in an edition of 500 copies in fall 2011 | Distributed in Canada by the Literary Press Group www.lpg.ca | Distributed in the United States by Small Press Distribution www.spdbooks.org | Shop on-line at www.bookthug.ca

Set in Nexus Serif.
Type & design by Malcolm Sutton.

If you have obtained this new edition of *Panopticon* through your favourite bookstore, there is an audio companion to the book that can be purchased at this link:

www.bookthug.ca/panopticonaudio